ARSENIC *and* OLD SILK

Mary Blount Christian

Annie's®

AnniesFiction.com

Library of Congress-in-Publication Data
Arsenic and Old Silk / by Mary Blount Christian
p. cm.
I. Title
                    2015957565

AnniesFiction.com
(800) 282-6643
Secrets of the Quilt™
Series Creator: Shari Lohner
Series Editors: Shari Lohner, Janice Tate, and Ken Tate
Cover Illustrator: Jonathan Bouw

10 11 12 13 14 | Printed in China | 9 8 7 6 5 4 3 2 1

Cabot Falls, Vermont
Present Day

$\mathcal{S}$ofia Parker shivered involuntarily as a sense of uneasiness overcame her. She couldn't shake the feeling that something was wrong. The kids should have been home already. Glancing up from the clutter of old sauce-stained recipes spread across her kitchen counter, she saw that the October dusk had closed in over Cabot Falls like a gray blanket. It happened quickly in Vermont this time of year.

A flush of anger tinged with concern warmed Sofia's face.

Shoving aside the recipes, she pulled her crimson cardigan closed and went in search of Jim. She found him grading math papers at the dining table.

"Vanessa and Matthew aren't back, and it's nearly dark," she said. "He only needed notebook paper. It shouldn't take this long. She knows I don't want her driving after dark. What if something's wrong?"

Jim set down his red pencil and pulled her to him. "She probably ran into a friend at the store. You know how fast darkness falls now."

His ability to assess situations calmly was one of the many things that had attracted her to him in college. His pragmatic nature complemented her often-impulsive one, but not this time. Sofia pushed away, irritated that he wasn't as concerned as she was. "Vanessa hasn't practiced night driving, Jim. Besides, I specifically told her not to dawdle. And if you're about to call me a 'smother hen,' don't!"

She stalked back to the kitchen. She considered calling Vanessa's cell phone, but she didn't want her driving and talking on the phone. *What good is that thing?* Ten minutes more, she told herself, and then she'd take Jim's car and go look for them.

Fergus, the border collie, padded in, head cocked, ears on the alert. He whimpered and wagged his tail, watching the door intently.

A bright beam of light crawled across the goldenrod-yellow wall as a car turned into the driveway. Sofia exhaled a deep breath of relief. Seconds later, the outside door was flung open so hard that it thudded loudly against the wall. Ten-year-old Matthew burst through the door with all the enthusiasm of a puppy. Fergus spun on his back legs, yipping.

"You should've seen it, Mom!" He shed his jacket and tossed it onto the counter. "That camera flashed when we went through the intersection. It was so cool." He bent down and rubbed Fergus under the chin.

"Camera?" Sofia handed him his jacket and nodded toward the hooks by the door. "What are you saying?"

"The Big Brother camera." Matthew hung his navy blue jacket without missing a beat. "That's what Vanessa called it. Zap! You know, the traffic camera on Main." He waved his newly purchased notebook paper.

Sofia understood all too well. It was the new traffic cam that took photos of cars crossing on red lights. She stood, hands on her hips and foot impatiently tapping, waiting.

Seventeen-year-old Vanessa removed her coat and hung it in one swift motion. She stopped short as her eyes met Sofia's. "I had to run the light." She glared at Matthew. "Blabbermouth. I told you to let me explain."

Sofia scooped up the recipes and shoved them back into their box. "What part did he get wrong? The part where you ran a red light? Or the part where the camera took the photo? Or maybe you mean the fine that will arrive here shortly."

"I can explain, Mom! I—I was trying to get away."

Jim stood in the doorway, leaning casually against the jamb. "Get away from what, Vanessa?"

"It was awesome!" Matthew interjected. "She's like a speed demon." He made a few karate chops in the air. "Zap! Pow!"

"I was not!" Vanessa said. "Just let me tell it, ninja boy." She shot him a warning look. "I was scared. We were being followed."

"Followed?" Sofia distinctly felt her heart skip a beat. "Are you sure?" She turned to her young son. "Matthew?"

He shrugged. "I didn't see it."

Vanessa rolled her eyes. "Of course you didn't. That's because you're so short. You couldn't see over the headrest."

"Don't call me short, Amazon."

"Stop it, you two," Sofia snapped. "Tell me what happened."

Tears welled in Vanessa's eyes. "The same dark SUV that was parked across from our cul-de-sac when I drove out was in the parking lot when we came out of the store. He—"

"He?" Jim interrupted. His forehead wrinkled. "Are you positive it was a man? Did you see him? Could you identify him? Did you get the license number?" He shot rapid-fire questions at her.

"No, no, and no." Vanessa crossed her arms defensively. "Mom, you always say if something feels wrong, it probably is. I just saw that the light was turning, and I figured I would make the best of it and run."

"This is Cabot Falls, not some crime-ridden big city," Sofia said, more to assure herself than to express fact. "I can accept that you thought you were followed and did what you thought was the right thing. But you broke the law, and—"

The timer on the oven buzzed. Sofia shut it off and grabbed her oven mitts. The sweet smells of basil and tomato permeated the kitchen as she lifted the lasagna casserole to the cork trivet on the counter. She inhaled deeply before turning to her daughter.

"It is your ticket to pay, Vanessa. If I didn't have more on my plate this month than I can manage alone, I'd take your keys. But I need all the help I can get, and that means letting you run some of the errands in my car."

October was a busy month for commitments. Sofia had promised Wynter's ninth-grade homeroom something "spectacular" for the cakewalk at the Halloween Carnival. She was also sponsoring a hot beverage stall for Vanessa's eleventh-grade class, and she had already paid a deposit for a booth at the Renaissance Festival. It would take the entire family helping to get through this month.

"I guess it would be a bad time to talk about a new dress for the Harvest Ball," Vanessa said.

Ah, youthful optimism, Sofia mused. "Yes, an extremely bad time. What about last year's dress?"

Vanessa grimaced. "That dress is so babyish."

"We'll see what we can do."

Vanessa sighed deeply.

Sofia ignored that and peeled back the foil on the bread, releasing a garlicky, buttery aroma. "Jim, if you'll clear your papers from the table please. Matthew, get Luke and Wynter. And Vanessa—"

"I'll get the plates and silverware, Mom." She was already grabbing the napkins and place mats.

Sofia set Fergus's food bowl next to his water and joined the family in the dining room. The Parkers' primary rule was never to take a problem to the table. Chatter turned from sinister stalkers to the lighter events of the day. The tense mood lessened considerably, but Sofia knew that it was only a lull in the storm.

She was sure that the rest of them realized it too, including Fergus, who launched into a barking fit while they were eating.

After dinner, when Sofia and Vanessa were cleaning up, Vanessa remained adamant that someone had been stalking her. Someone in a dark SUV, of all things. It sounded so sinister. *But what if she's right?* The chill of goose bumps crept up Sofia's spine and made the hairs on the back of her neck stand up.

Jim was still grading papers when Sofia set the security alarm and turned out the kitchen light. The younger Parkers had retired to their rooms and homework. Sofia settled into her favorite wing chair and flipped on the reading lamp. She picked up the antique diary, relishing the feel of the leather cover worn soft through the touch of many hands as it passed through the generations.

Nonna—Sofia's grandmother Elena Baresi—had willed the diary along with the family's prized heirloom quilt to Sofia, the youngest and least talented in needlecraft of the three sisters. Their mother had died when Sofia was four. Nonna had two other daughters, and they had daughters. Yet she had left the quilt's guardianship to Sofia.

The fabrics, spanning six centuries and at least two continents, held a history of famous people—artists, authors, kings, and statesmen who had profoundly changed the world. It was also a history of her ancestors who had touched those lives in significant ways. It made the fragile heirloom priceless. But Nonna had always insisted that it remain in the family, hidden from view.

No one had been more surprised by the bequest than Sofia. She was determined to study the diary that explained the origins of the squares until she learned about every one of her ancestors who'd contributed to it. It was a project that her sisters and aunts understood and supported.

The stories she had uncovered about humble lives bravely lived, like the individual squares when pieced together, made the whole creation strong and meaningful. She was learning that although her life when compared with her sisters' lives seemed less notable, she, too, touched people in her own unique way. Perhaps that was why Nonna had chosen her as the guardian—to dispel once and for all her feeling that she had somehow failed to reach her potential.

She opened the diary and thumbed through it until she found the entry for the fifth square. The quilt block in question reminded her of the first pale green sprigs that break through the brittle ground in the spring. It was a green that spoke of hope and promise, a nice contrast to the bleak and colorless October landscape out her window.

Sofia tugged the Highland plaid lap throw higher around her shoulders and slowly translated the delicate Italian handwriting: *Maddalena Vitari, Windsor Castle, London, England, 1536.*

She didn't need her dual-language dictionary to understand the gist of the message as she scanned the page, snatching at words hidden in the text like wildflowers in a field of weeds. Sofia had accompanied Nonna on her visit to Italy and remained for a year afterward to study the cuisine, but she had forgotten most of the language she had picked up there and from Nonna. She was relearning, thanks to online translation sites. But it was a slow process, which meant her English-Italian dictionary was never far away when she was reading the diary.

Morte sospetta, "suspicious death"; *decapitato*, "beheaded"; and *veleno*, "poison." The words caught Sofia by surprise. She stared at the page. *Re Enrico VIII.* "King Henry VIII"? What was a nice Italian girl doing hanging out with English royalty?

Sofia puzzled over the incongruences of an Italian woman linked with someone as notorious as Henry VIII. Add to that the sixteenth-century date, and the puzzle grew deeper. There must have been some error.

"*A chi vuole, non mancano modi,*" Sofia murmured, quoting one of Nonna's favorite sayings aloud.

"And what does that mean?"

Sofia startled at the sound of Jim's voice. He stood next to her, grinning. She smiled up at the face that still thrilled her. "It means 'Where there is a will, there is a way.'"

"Aha!" Jim said, pointing skyward. "I *will* that we go to bed. There is a *way* up the stairs." He offered her his hand, and Sofia allowed him to pull her to a standing position. She flipped off the reading lamp, and the hall light cut a bright slash across the floor.

Immediately she was back in the twenty-first century with dark SUVs and stalkers. "Hang on a second," she said, almost apologetically. She rechecked the alarm and then went to the window and peered into the darkness. The lone streetlight cast an eerie glow through the mist that thickened in the night, like a cloud descended to earth. There were no telltale signs of dull light bouncing off of dark metal, no sinister silhouettes creeping about. She rattled the doorknob to reassure herself that it was securely locked. "Okay, I'm done." She trusted Fergus to alert them of anything more suspicious than a raccoon.

"Are you worried about Vanessa's stalker?" Jim asked, leading her up the steps.

"Aren't you?"

"It was probably nothing more than her imagination. And when she has to work to pay off her ticket, that'll make her think twice before running a light again."

Sofia yawned, realizing for the first time that she was truly exhausted, physically and emotionally. "You're probably right, *cara mia.*" At least she hoped so. "That clock alarm will be blasting in our ears all too soon."

Sofia wrestled with the cover half the night, and her pillow turned into a lump of rocks. She struggled to find a comfortable position, finally accomplishing that about the time the alarm went off.

Then it was a rush to get everyone dressed, fed, and out the door with a hug, kiss, and good wishes. Sofia collapsed into her chair with a cup of cocoa and proceeded to make out her shopping list. She checked her coupons and found she had a few that were applicable. By the time she transferred a pot roast from the freezer to the fridge for slow thawing, the clock indicated the grocer would be open for business.

Grabbing her jacket from the hall closet, she stepped onto the front stoop and paused, inhaling the sweet smell of burning wood. A thin wisp of smoke curled from the Coopers' chimney across the cul-de-sac.

"Hello, Sofia," Pat Cooper called out.

"Oh, I didn't see you hunkered over your flower bed . . . Pat." Sofia almost visibly winced. They'd been neighbors for more than a decade, but before that, they had been teacher and student. It was still weird to call her Pat instead of Mrs. Cooper. And although Sofia was confident in her grammar usage, she always felt a bit awkward talking to her, as if she expected to be graded at the close of the conversation. The woman took no notice, however. She was more wrapped up in her flowers and her television shows, especially the law enforcement programs.

Pat Cooper picked up a pot and strolled over with her poodle, Willow, trotting at her heels. She handed the flowerpot to Sofia. "Here, I overbought, as usual. Take some of these pansies. Don't worry; you can just leave them alone. They don't take much attention, and their little faces are so cute when they bloom."

"Thank you. As always, you'll have the prettiest yard in the neighborhood next year." She fingered the delicate young leaves that reminded her of the fifth quilt square.

"There's not a lot else to do right now. Homer is still typing away on his history of the world. I don't know why he insisted that I retire with him. I had a few more good years to give. Eighty is the new fifty, you know. All the experts say so. Look at those gorgeous NCIS agents with the white hair on television. They're still working. And they get their perps every week. They show those young ones a thing or two."

Sofia smiled at Pat's use of cop slang. "Although that's fictional."

Pat stepped closer and lowered her voice. She looked around before she spoke. "Maybe, but I thought we were in for a real 594 last night, or at least a 211."

Sofia didn't like it when her neighbor took that cryptic tone. It sounded like trouble. After Vanessa's story about someone following her, she felt weak in the knees. "I'm sorry, Pat. I don't speak police code. What do you mean?"

Pat seemed lost in her own thoughts for a moment, no doubt relishing the vision of herself as a gray-haired detective. "A 594 is malicious mischief, and 211 is a robbery in progress—at least that's what I've gathered from my police programs. Homer's always fussing at me to get away from the window, but if I didn't look out once in a while, there's no telling what I might miss."

"What about last night?" Sofia could feel her patience giving way to anxiety.

"There was a dark SUV circling the cul-de-sac slowly, as if the driver was looking for a special address. I couldn't tell if it was dark blue or black. I grew suspicious when it circled two more times. I pulled back the drapes so the driver could see that I had my phone, and he sped away."

Sofia felt as if her legs might buckle, and she stepped back to brace her body against the doorframe. "What time was this? Do you know?"

"Of course I know. I jotted it down, just in case." Pat pulled a pocket notebook from her back jeans pocket and read: "'7:12 p.m., unsub'—that's unidentified subject—'circles cul-de-sac three times, makes quick getaway when spotted.'" She shoved the notebook back into her pocket. "I didn't get a license plate."

Sofia bit her lip, remembering. That would have been while they were having dinner. She recalled having to stop Fergus from a barking fit. Had he heard the SUV circling the cul-de-sac and then speeding away? Had someone followed Vanessa after all? Was it the same driver who had been parked across the street when she left? Was her daughter in danger?

2

Venice, Italy
Autumn 1532

Merchant ships and Chinese junks, their sails furled to their masts, bobbed to the heartbeat of Venice's turquoise lagoon. The first hint of pink and yellow spread across the western sky on this autumn day. It would be dark soon.

Standing on the pier in front of her easel, Maddalena frowned in disappointment. She dropped her paintbrush into the vial of turpentine. Why could she not put on canvas what her eyes saw and what her heart felt? *How can I even consider myself an artist with such inferior work?* She groaned, consoling herself that perhaps a troubled heart was too difficult a burden to ignore. All day she had restrained herself from admitting her fears to Allessandro. She could no longer keep silent.

Maddalena perched herself on a pylon and gazed at Allessandro. He was lost in his own painting. His strong, chiseled jaw and straight nose created a handsome profile. She had loved him since they were children. Now, as she approached her majority, she daydreamed of marrying him despite Papa's objections. "I am frightened, Allessandro. Something is wrong at home. I can feel trouble in the air."

Allessandro's head jerked at the sound of her voice as if he had forgotten that she was there. "You mean aside from your father's intense dislike for me?" He put down his brush and sat beside her, taking her hand in his. *"Dolor comunicato è subito scemato*—a problem shared is a problem halved. Tell me."

The warmth of his gentle touch gave her the strength to speak. "Papa has been quiet of late. Eerily quiet. That is not like him. But I see him watching me. His eyes are cold, expressionless." Maddalena struggled for words that reflected the instinct she felt. "He is planning something bad. I feel it, and it frightens me."

"Perhaps you misunderstand," Allessandro suggested. "He is your father. Do not let your vivid imagination get the best of you."

She shook her head vigorously. "He cares nothing for my happiness, only for his prestige in Venice and with his clients. He cares more for one of his Murano bowls or his Oriental vases."

A successful merchant of fine fabrics, laces, and notions, Orsino Vitari had amassed a fortune, which he flaunted with the finest furnishings and artifacts. Their palace was a showplace of riches that would never be hers. To him, she was only a living mannequin on which to display his wares in the latest fashions.

Not that any of his *ricchezza* meant anything to her. It bought her no happiness. Venetian women were denied education except for sewing, weaving, and running a household for their husbands. They owned nothing but their dowries, for which they were expected to remain chaste, modest, silent, and obedient. It was with the latter two that Maddalena had the most trouble.

"Venice accepts women as poets and writers," she had argued with Papa. "Why is it so wrong for us to tell stories with paint? Even courtesans have more freedom and exposure to the arts. It is unfair!" She spoke her mind on the matter and read her father's books in secret when he was on his long trips. She was not to be denied.

Allessandro cupped her chin and turned her to face him. His eyes met hers. "When you reach your majority, we will marry. By then I—"

"You know that Papa will never accept you." Tears blurred her vision. "He will see that the *Scuola* won't either." As a friend and confidant of the *doge*—the chief magistrate—of Venice, Orsino Vitari commanded influence.

Maddalena's shoulders sagged in defeat. Only members of the *Scuola di Venetian Arte* were allowed to sell their paintings. Without patrons, Allessandro would remain unrecognized. Not that his status mattered to her. "Let us stow away on one of those ships, Allessandro. Wherever it goes, it must be better than here under Papa's watchful eyes. What about the New World?"

Allessandro smiled, his teeth brilliant white against his olive skin. "I love you, Maddalena. But your father plans a life of privilege for you. I can offer you only the charities parceled out by the wealthy until I am allowed to sell my paintings. How will I ever do that if no one of influence sponsors me?"

The pink and purple sky was quickly turning indigo. Maddalena squeezed the liquid from her brush. "I must go before Papa finds me here," she said moments before heavy footsteps approached on the pier. Maddalena turned her head toward the sound. "Papa!" She turned back to her companion. "Remember, Alle, no matter what happens, I love you with all my heart." She hopped down from her perch on the pylon, snatched her canvas and paints, and scampered to meet her father.

"You intolerable child! You defy me the moment I turn my back." He spun on his heel.

"Papa, we only paint together. The dock has so many wonderful things to paint." She fell into step behind him, stumbling as she tried to keep up.

"Bah! You will pursue the feminine arts. And you will forget that boy." He pushed against the ornate wrought iron gate to their property. It made a rasping sound as he flung it open and stomped past the stone statues. Papa pushed open the carved wooden door to their palace with such force that it slammed against the wall. The portrait of her mother fell to the marble floor, chipping a corner of the gold leaf frame.

Maddalena leaned her canvas against the wall and rehung the portrait. If only Mama had lived, perhaps she could have interceded. She stared at the portrait of the wistful-eyed young woman with flowing dark hair and wondered if she had loved Papa. *Was he always so unbending?*

"Change your clothes," her father snapped. "It is nearly time for dinner."

Maddalena entered the dining room a short while later and took her place at the far end of the long oak table. The high-back chair was so overpowering that she felt dwarfed by it. Her view of Papa was all but blocked by the tall tapered candles jutting from the pair of silver candelabra.

She shook her napkin open and placed it on her lap as Zaneta Sorbello, the rotund cook, bustled into the dining room with a platter of antipasti and prosecco wine. It effervesced as she poured it into the long-stem glasses etched with a bold *V*.

When Zaneta exited, Papa set down his glass. "I have secured a tutor in French and English for you. She will begin tomorrow."

"Why French and English, Papa? They are useless to me." Maddalena twisted in her chair, trying to see his expression through the candles. "Why can't I study the stars or history, Papa?" She wondered if this was punishment to keep her from painting and from Allessandro. She decided that this was the reason for his silence these last weeks.

"You will go with me on my next trip," Papa said. "It is time for you to see that there is more than Venice." He rang the sterling bell. "You have little time before we leave."

Before Maddalena could respond, Zaneta rushed in to collect the remaining antipasti and refresh the wine glasses. She quickly returned with peas, ham, and risotto with ink-blackened cuttlefish.

Maddalena waved her off. She had no appetite. Papa's trips always took months, and she had looked forward to the freedom she felt when he was gone. A part of her was excited. She had never been beyond the canals and bridges connecting the islands of Venice. As a child, she had sat at his feet as he spoke of the English king's palace.

"Do I have a choice, Papa?" she asked. *Why do I feel such impending doom? How can I bear to be away from Allessandro so long?*

"No." His voice was firm.

In the following days, the tutor drilled Maddalena on languages and English etiquette. "Bring the right foot gently, smoothly behind your left so that it is at an angle. With your head bowed, bend your knees and at the waist."

Maddalena tried to curtsy for the hundredth time that afternoon.

"No no no, child! Control your arms. You are not a bird about to fly away."

"I do not want to bow to some Englishman," Maddalena said. "I am Venetian."

"He is not 'some Englishman,' child. He is the king." The tutor threw her hands up. "You will not likely see him anyway. Look at the floor when you bow your head."

Every afternoon, Maddalena had to sit quietly and embroider, which Papa said was more fitting for a woman than painting. "Slowly, child, and smaller stitches. This is not a race. Pause and let your needle dangle loose so that your thread does not twist," the *signora* pleaded as she grew more and more exasperated with her wayward student.

Maddalena tried to imagine the thread as oil paint and the needle as her brush. It made the task more tolerable. If she was careful, she could mimic the smooth velvet look of the oils. In fact, she found she was quite good at the craft when she focused. But it was not nearly as enjoyable to her as painting.

Papa was at his warehouse most of the day, but the tutor kept Maddalena too busy to leave the house—no doubt on Papa's orders. When she wasn't studying or sewing, the seamstress who was creating her travel wardrobe, a showpiece of Papa's fabrics, insisted on numerous fittings. Maddalena was a prisoner in her own home.

On the sixth day she overheard Papa tell Zaneta that they would be leaving in two days. She feigned a headache, slipped through her window, and made her way to where Allessandro would be painting.

His face glistened, and he wiped it with his sleeve. "Maddalena!" He smiled and opened his arms invitingly.

She threw her arms around him. "Oh, Alle, Papa is taking me with him on his trip. I will write you every day, even if I cannot always send my letters. Do not forget me, cara mia."

He cupped her face in his hands and kissed her tenderly. "You will see wonderful things. Remember them all so that I may see through your eyes." His voice was buoyant with cheeriness, but his eyes mirrored the sadness she felt.

For many days, smaller boats had carried bolts of *broccatello, drappo d'oro, damasco, velluto,* and *lampasso* fabrics in colors of grass, sky, and sunsets to the galleon in which they'd sail to England. Some fabrics bore the intricate designs of birds, medallions, and flowers stamped or skillfully cut by Venetian artisans. They took also bobbins of lace and metal thread packed in barrels.

Although Maddalena had painted many seascapes with the merchant ships, this was the first time she had ever actually been on the deck of one. She stood to one side as the sailors heaved the anchor aboard and marveled as they scrambled up the mast and onto the arms, removing the ties that held the sails. The white cloth unfurled like the wings of a bird and swelled with the wind. Their metal rings clinked, and the ship creaked and groaned as it rocked with the waves.

Maddalena stood at the stern of the galleon and watched as her beloved Venice grew smaller.

They sailed south to the Mediterranean Sea and up again, hugging the coastlines of France and Spain, with port stops for fresh supplies. Papa kept Maddalena busy clipping samples of the fabrics and sketching popular fashions of the day.

He smiled a good deal more, and Maddalena felt much closer to him. Yet sometimes, if she turned quickly, she caught an expression on his face so dark that it made goose bumps crawl up her arms. She had always accepted that fathers loved their daughters. It may have been true when she was a little girl. Now she was not so sure. She thought it was because she grew to look more like her mother with each passing day. Yet the look on his face did not seem like sadness, only raw anger.

It seemed forever to Maddalena before they at last entered the waters between France and England. "The French call it *La Manche,*" Papa told her, "because it resembles a sleeve. The English call it the English Channel. What you see through the telescope is England. Above those white cliffs is Dover. There we will transfer the goods to wagons for a four-day journey to Windsor Castle in Berkshire County west of London."

It took a day to transfer the crates and bolts from the ship to the waiting wagons. The port was noisy with merchants and travelers in all manner of dress, selling and bargaining and arguing. Maddalena kept herself occupied by sketching the interesting faces and activities she saw.

Finally, they left behind the noise of Dover and traveled by caravan. Before dusk they stopped, and the men set up two tents, one for Maddalena and one for her father. Despite the October chill, the others slept outdoors, some under the wagons after they hobbled the horses to graze.

The trees were barren, and the ground was brittle and hard. Already the excitement of the adventure was gone. England seemed gray and sad. Maddalena longed for the sound of lapping water and the warmth of the sun reflecting off the yellow stone palaces. The roads were rutted and bumpy, and occasionally the entire caravan paused to repair a broken wheel or for Papa to negotiate a toll fee to pass. He said that the bridge keeper was appointed to keep it passable, and the king allowed him to charge passersby. The king took his share in taxes. With bridges all over England, the king could well afford to buy Papa's fabrics.

Maddalena sketched the travelers they met along the way—merchants with fine horses, pedestrians with baskets of vegetables on their backs, and curious children who stared at the caravan, then went back to their games. She saw dark-skinned men in long robes with their heads wrapped in fabric leading horses with saddlebags brimming with oils and perfumes. She saw a woman in a colorful dress with hoops of gold hanging from her ears and necklaces that caught the glint of the morning sun. She carried a swaddled baby, and a little dog ran yapping at her feet. Now and then, a man wearing a tunic that bore an embroidered crest plodded along on his Spanish jennet or Irish hobby.

It was their third day on land when Maddalena became aware of a din of noise as they moved forward. Ahead loomed what looked like a city—London. It reminded her of the Venetian squares, and a wave of homesickness swept over her.

To her disappointment, the caravan continued past London for a full day as it traveled along the River Thames to Windsor. Papa pointed to the massive structure up a steep hill that dwarfed the rows of little houses, pubs, and inns lining the river's banks. He said it was only the outer wall they were looking at. The palace was inside along with a massive courtyard, chapels, buildings, and apartments where royalty, ambassadors, their assistants, and servants stayed.

"Hundreds of people live there at one time—ambassadors from other countries, visitors like us, and families of those who serve at the king's pleasure. You will see. Tomorrow we will take our fabrics to show. You will meet the tailors and seamstresses who keep the king's court clothed." His mood lightened considerably.

Orsino Vitari was successful in selling all of his fabrics, as he had predicted. The monarchs and nobles were drawn to the reds and purples, which they considered regal.

The seamstresses bought Maddalena's favorite, a pale silver-green silk like the first fragile leaves of spring. They crowded around, handling the fabric and chattering brightly. One of the ladies introduced Maddalena to the gaggle. Unfamiliar as she was with the harsh sounds of the English words, she could not imagine being called Alice or Rose or Lucy.

Mabel Swan, the seamstress in charge, was tall and thin with skin stretched taut over her skull. After finishing her transaction with Papa, she stood with hands on her hips and regarded Maddalena with sunken, dark eyes like deep pits. Without warning and stealthily as a pickpocket, the older woman snatched the book of Maddalena's sketches and flipped through it with fingers calloused from years working at her craft. Maddalena stood in shocked silence, wondering if Mabel Swan was as scary as she looked.

Another woman, who looked as old as Mabel but had no apparent authority, smiled sweetly at Maddalena, cocking her head and nodding rhythmically until Mabel snapped at her to get busy. She hustled back inside, and Maddalena watched through the windows as she took her place and got back to work. She held the material close to her cloudy eyes, likely weakened by years of eyestrain. It was yet another reason Maddalena preferred painting to sewing.

When the wagons were empty, Papa released them. It was time to start for home. With no burden but their personal belongings, they could make better time traveling by carriage across France and Switzerland, then down to Turin and over to Venice. They would be home by Christmas. Maddalena all but skipped, her feet felt so light.

Home! Allessandro. Soon.

It was still dark when she awoke the next day. She dressed quickly, anxious to be on the road toward Dover.

"*Buondì*, Papa, good morning," she greeted him outside where he was watching the men ready the carriage. "I am ready." It was a chilly morning, and she wrapped herself a bit more tightly in her traveling cloak.

"You will not be returning with me," he muttered. He did not look at her.

"Of course I will be," she said calmly, although panic was rising in her chest.

"No, Maddalena."

"I am your only daughter. I can't stay here," she said, but her heart sank. She knew he spoke the truth.

"When I have arranged a proper marriage for you with a substantial husband, I will send for you. Until then, you will remain at Windsor. You will work as a seamstress, you will offer no trouble, and you will forget that boy."

"Papa! You cannot do this to me." But she was sure that this had been his plan all along.

"I can and will, you ungrateful girl. You will sew for the king until I return for you." He turned on his heel to leave.

Maddalena grabbed his arm, but he brushed her away with such force that she was thrown off balance and fell facedown, weeping. "Papa!"

Her father climbed into the dark cab of the carriage. The pair of ebony jennets lurched forward. Her lips formed a plea, but no sound came. She lay on the ground, weeping.

She felt the sharp jab of a shoe in her ribs. It was Mabel Swan, the leading seamstress. Her thin lips turned down in a sour expression. "Get up!"

Maddalena struggled to her feet. Still shaken by her father's betrayal, she clamped her lips together to keep them from trembling.

Mabel crossed her arms. "You are no longer Maddalena. You will answer to the English name Margaret. You will speak English only. You will serve at my pleasure. Disobedience will not be tolerated. Do you understand? You are *mine*."

Out of the corner of her eye, Maddalena saw the black carriage pass through the gate and out of sight. She had but one goal now. Survival.

3

Cabot Falls, Vermont
Present Day

Surviving this overbooked month with good humor was going to be rough. There was no room in October for mysterious stalkers. Sofia was relieved when several days passed without incident, convincing her that the dark SUV Vanessa and Pat had seen was only an out-of-towner lost in an unfamiliar area.

Sofia drove to the library with no more on her mind than the bright red sports car tailgating her Chevy Suburban until it sped away, leaving the acrid smell of exhaust to seep through the open vent. At the library, she went straight to the front desk, where her good friend and the head librarian, Marla Dixon, was waiting for her with a stack of books. Usually Sofia liked to browse the shelves awhile, but she was grateful that she could rely on Marla to get her in and out when she was in a hurry.

Back home in record time, Sofia set the library books on the stand by her reading lamp, kicked off her cognac suede ankle boots, and slipped into her espadrilles. Marla had gathered a selection of Renaissance books for Sofia. They would not only give her some ideas for the festival but could also offer some insight into her research about her ancestor, Maddalena Vitari.

Sofia brewed herself a cup of tea, settled herself in her favorite chair, and picked up a book about Henry VIII. There was nothing more satisfying than resting a hardcover book between her hands. The oil-rich aroma of the ink lingered long after it was read by many pairs of eyes, and the feel of a page between her fingers was far more satisfying than clicking and scrolling and swiping.

In the kitchen to stretch her legs and put her mug in the dishwasher, Sofia saw the message light flashing on the house phone. The voice sounded so young that at first she thought it might be a prank.

"I didn't know that I was supposed to do a shower until . . . well, I just didn't know stuff like that. I need you to cater a shower luncheon. Oh, I'm Gretchen Wingate." The message ended with a phone number and three rapid-fire pleases.

Sofia dialed the number; she felt terrible about it, but she would have to tell the girl that she couldn't take on another project until after New Year's.

Gretchen answered on the first ring. "Oh, thank you, thank you. My mom is, like, ready to ground me forever. My social life will be over if I don't fix this."

Sofia took pity on the girl and decided to hear her out. "When is the wedding?" Maybe she could steer her in the right direction.

"They're marrying on the thirtieth."

"This month? Well, I can't help you, but—"

"No. But you *have* to! Please, please, *please*?" Gretchen sounded nearly hysterical. "Just a soup, salad, and, like, little sandwiches, my mom said. And a few pumpkins and stuff—you know."

Sofia set down her pencil. "Pumpkins? For a bridal lunch?"

"Yeah, they're wearing Halloween costumes for the wedding. It's going to be so cute, really unforgettable."

Sofia muffled a giggle. *Unforgettable is right!* Before the conversation ended, she had committed to securing the tables, chairs, decorations, and food. As Gretchen chattered on, she kept adding to the number of people. Sofia had no sooner hung up than the phone rang again and Gretchen said, "I forgot to add me and my mom. Oh, and the mother of the bride."

"Did you include the mother of the groom?" Sofia asked.

"I guess I should, shouldn't I? Do you send out the invitations too?"

Sofia rolled her eyes, Wynter-style. "That's on you, and you should do it, *like*, yesterday."

When she hung up the phone, she had one of those aha moments she cherished. *Bride-and-groom pumpkin heads!* This project could actually be fun—and just the thing for Vanessa to earn a little money toward her traffic fine.

The thought of Vanessa brought back images of a dark SUV, its driver obscured from view behind smoky gray windows. She fervently hoped that Vanessa was being paranoid. But her neighbor's comments didn't support that theory. Pat had said that she observed the driver slowly circle several times around the cul-de-sac and then speed away when she made herself known. It was suspicious. Sofia glanced at the alarm pad to reassure herself it was set.

She realized that she would suspect every delivery driver and soccer mom in a dark SUV from now on. She wouldn't drive anywhere without one eye on her rearview mirror.

Almost without thinking, she went to the window and looked out. There was no sign of a strange vehicle. Of course, her car was in plain view in the driveway. And Vanessa was safely tucked away in school.

The phone rang again and Sofia groaned. How many more people was Gretchen going to add to the list?

"You are in danger," an unfamiliar voice said. The words sounded muffled and hollow, as if they were spoken from a deep well.

Sofia felt her blood turn to ice.

"Your family is not safe."

Sofia slammed down the phone and grabbed her keys. If Vanessa was the target, then the predator would go to the school. Sofia glanced at the mantel clock. It was almost dismissal time. She quickly tapped in her alarm code to allow her to exit and then reset it and ran outside without a jacket, ignoring the chill. Fergus had eagerly joined her, jumping into the Suburban when she opened the door and settling into the passenger seat as she pulled out of the driveway. What if the stalker was at the school, waiting?

Windsor, England
Autumn 1532

Maddalena trembled from rage and fear. Had her father really left her at Windsor Castle to work for this monster, Mabel Swan? She tried to pull away, but the woman's grip on her arm was too firm. "Let go of me! Papa will be back for me at any moment. He was just trying to teach me a lesson, that's all."

"Little fool," Mabel scoffed. "He is not coming back. I haven't time for this. There is work to be done, Margaret."

"Don't call me that. I am Maddalena Vitari, daughter of Orsino Vitari of the Republic of Venice." Tears splashed onto her cheeks. How could he do this? It was like a slap in the face. She had never felt more betrayed and alone. She knew nothing of survival on her own.

Maddalena could not erase the image of her father's carriage leaving her behind or Mabel Swan's cold pronouncement, "You are mine." As the highest-ranking seamstress, Mabel had power, which meant there was no recourse for Maddalena. Her arm lost feeling, and she ceased struggling.

"You should be honored to serve King Henry," Mabel lectured, pulling her along the corridor past women in coarse wool smocks the color of mud who were scrubbing the soot-stained walls. "First we must get you dressed properly."

"What's wrong with my clothes?" Maddalena demanded.

"They are a violation of sumptuary law. Only monarchs and nobles may wear velvet, furs, silk, lace, cottons, and taffeta. Even your colors are reprehensible." Mabel pushed her through a doorway into a small, dark room adjacent to the fabric vault. "Remove your clothes—now!"

Maddalena undressed slowly and tossed her fine clothes to the floor.

Crossing her arms, Mabel added, "The farthingale too." She pointed to a gray linen gown and kirtle folded on the table. "Those are for you. From now on, the only fabrics you may wear are wool and linen. Sheepskin is permissible for warmth."

"In Venice, even the poor wear beautiful clothes," Maddalena protested. Because styles changed rapidly, the wealthy gave their clothes to the charities. The practice had made Venice a fashionable city and Papa a wealthy man.

Mabel shrugged indifferently. "You are not in Venice anymore, nor will you be for a long time, if ever."

Maddalena felt as if a knife had been thrust into her heart. Had Mabel Swan really said "if ever"? Could Papa really hate her that much?

Mabel's mouth crooked into a smirk. "Not so haughty now, are you, missy?" She motioned toward a door. "Get in there."

Filled with fear and apprehension, Maddalena looked around the plain, sparsely furnished room, bright with sunlight streaming through the row of windows. Was it only yesterday that she had stood on this very spot and watched these women hunched over their sewing? It seemed a lifetime ago. Was it really possible that she was now to become one of them?

Mabel retrieved a long rod that leaned against the doorframe and tapped the floor with it. "Ladies, Margaret is joining us."

Only one of them looked up from her work. Lucy Creket was as plump as a baby and seemed blissfully unaware that she was of less value than the needle she held. She was an apprentice seamstress who practiced the art of simultaneously stitching and chattering like a magpie. "Well, if it ain't Mistress 'igh-and-Mighty," she said. "Only yesterday you toured the palace like an honored guest. And 'ere you are, no better than the rest of us." Her taunting laugh sounded like a cackling hen.

"Silence!" Mabel snapped. She struck the side of Lucy's bench with her rod with a loud bang. Lucy turned the corners of her mouth down and wagged her head from side to side without missing a stitch.

"Give your project to Margaret," Mabel instructed the oldest in the group.

The one called Alice Thorpe moved over to share her bench. "Sit here, Margaret," she said. Her face was a road map of disappointment and pain, and her eyes darted like those of a trapped animal. Maddalena guessed that although her skin resembled old parchment, Alice was probably no more than thirty-five, about the same as Mabel.

Maddalena settled herself on the hard seat. The linen clothes were stiff and scratched her skin. She was not surprised that most of these women wore pained expressions. This place would lead you to believe there was no comfort at all in the world.

Alice handed a white silk tunic to Maddalena. "The hem is half done. You can finish this, and I'll start on another." She patted Maddalena's hand reassuringly. "Everything will be fine."

"I expect to see progress on these garments when I return," Mabel said. She turned on her heel and swept from the room.

Maddalena sat next to Alice and observed the others. It was obvious that the sewing circle had its barnyard pecking order. Lucy seemed to be the resident eavesdropper and gossip, her finger on the pulse of both royal and more mundane lives. She teased her fellow workers about their personal lives in one breath and shared tidbits about members of court in the next.

"Whose tunic is it?" Maddalena asked Alice. If Mabel had told her the truth about forbidden fabrics, she guessed it belonged to a royal or a lady.

Alice clasped her hands and cocked her head as if visualizing the scene. "It's for Queen Catherine to wear to the Christmas pageant. Everyone in the court will wear clothes to match her. The king has commissioned a play for the court and all the foreign dignitaries. There will be singing and dancing and entertainment and—"

Lucy laughed. "Alice, you talk like you've seen one, and we all know that ain't true."

"I did." Alice straightened her shoulders. "I peeked from behind a drape and saw them, all so beautiful in the silver and white finery we sewed. They had carnival masks with streamers too. And I heard the king sing a song he wrote. It was grand. Queen Catherine's costume was trimmed in white fur on the sleeves."

"Well, not anymore," Lucy said. "Sewing her gown is a waste of stitching time. 'Er grace is shut away in her apartments ever since the king brought her back. The Spanish ambassador is pleading her case."

"Shush, Lucy, the royal family's business is none of yours," Alice cautioned. "The walls have ears."

"All I'm saying is 'er days are numbered. That's what I'm saying. It ain't the queen sitting at 'is side no more," Lucy said. "It's that Boleyn courtesan, that's who."

"If I was the queen, I'd scratch her eyes out," the youngest seamstress interrupted. Had it not been for her perpetual frown, the girl would have been pretty, with blue eyes and dark brown hair peeking from beneath her cap.

"That's what you'd do if you saw Thom Bell with another?" Lucy asked.

Rose gave Lucy a murderous glare.

Lucy ignored her and went on to tell the newcomer all about how Rose Styles had worked there for two years, since her mother died. Lucy, now just sixteen, also had her eye on Thom Bell, a butcher in the royal kitchen. "Hands off him," Lucy warned Maddalena with a wink. "Rose has a nasty temper—and a dagger."

"I have no desire to meet Thom Bell. I am promised to Allessandro," Maddalena responded. She was bold enough to stick up for herself but not to ask about the Boleyn woman and why Queen Catherine was not living at the palace.

Lucy laughed. "'Ow long do you think your Allessandro will wait for you?"

"You are cruel, Lucy Creket." Maddalena flung the gown onto the bench and fled out the door and down the corridor, weaving between pedestrians until she was out of breath. She stopped to compose herself and realized that she was lost—and in big trouble if Mabel found out she was gone. "But I am not one of them," she mumbled. But she was, for now. Filled with frustration and anger, she turned to go back and ran straight into a boy. The impact sent them both sprawling to the stone floor.

He wore dark hose and britches. His plain silk smock was sweat-stained, and his ruddy cheeks stood out against his pale ivory skin. He ran his fingers through his hair, which was the color of ginger, and then he scrambled to his feet and offered her a hand. "So sorry. My fault," he apologized.

"I am equally to blame. My name is Mad—" She caught herself. "Margaret."

He laughed. "Your accent—it's Italian, Mad Margaret?"

She flushed at his teasing. "The Republic of Venice," she said. "Oh! Your smock is torn. Did I do that? Will that get you into trouble?" She glanced around fearfully. "Why do you dare flaunt silk so boldly? Are you new here too? You can be punished for such arrogance, I'm told."

His eyes danced with mischief. "Within an inch of my life, I am sure." He smiled at her and swept the air with his hand as he stepped aside. "I believe you were in a hurry."

Without responding, she raced toward the now-familiar door of the sewing room, dreading the wrath of Mabel Swan.

When she returned, Lucy cackled theatrically. "You lead a charmed life, you do, Margaret. Mabel ain't come back. You best look busy when she does if you don't want the rod across your back."

It seemed like good advice. Maddalena flopped back onto the bench and resumed hemming the silk gown.

"You have to ask Mabel's permission to leave," Rose said.

"She probably wanted to sneak to the kitchen to get a look at Thom," Lucy teased. She threw her head back and laughed.

Rose threw down the sleeve she was stitching and dove toward Lucy with her hands outstretched just as Mabel swept through the door. Rose quickly retreated back to her spot and started sewing again. "Later," she muttered under her breath.

Lucy laughed and looked unconcerned, but Maddalena caught a bit of worry behind her eyes.

At the end of her first day, Maddalena knew a little about each of the seamstresses. Rose and Lucy, like Mabel Swan, would make dangerous enemies, each in her own way. She knew to be wary of them. Only Alice seemed harmless enough, although the others called her daft.

"Alice, do we sleep here at Windsor in a dormitory or something?" Maddalena asked. "Where do we eat? Papa left me with nothing. I don't know what to do." She did not want to admit that she was terrified.

"I will take care of you like a daughter," Alice told her. "Come home with me."

Lucy whispered, "Don't trust Alice. She's full of cracks." But Maddalena gratefully followed Alice through the courtyard, out the gate, down the steep hill, and past a row of houses to a tavern, the King's Arms Inn. By that time, the last of the sun had disappeared. The cold penetrated her bones until she shivered uncontrollably.

Loud voices and lilting lyre music spilled into the alley as Alice led her around the side and to a small structure behind the tavern that might have been storage at one time. Still, it had a sturdy door that kept the cold out.

They had scarcely arrived when Alice disappeared out the door, saying she would be right back. Left alone in the small room, Maddalena took note of the cheery quilts that were draped about. She looked closely at one and suspected it had been sewn from scraps Alice had secreted away. Maddalena admired Alice's handiwork and her industriousness to make something so beautiful from shreds and tatters.

Before Maddalena had time to worry about being left alone in a storage shed, Alice returned with two steaming bowls of stew. The meat and turnips were simple and bland, but it was fresh and hot.

When Alice finished her meal, she put together a makeshift bed in the corner of the room. Maddalena wasn't sure where Alice got the energy. She was falling asleep over the last of her stew.

Alice took Maddalena's bowl and trundled her off to bed with a quilt and sheep's skin to protect her from the cold. Maddalena wrapped herself up and grasped the cross that hung around her neck for comfort. It was all she had to remind her of her mother.

What will Allessandro think when I do not return with Papa? That was her last thought before she fell asleep.

She dreamed of Zaneta's tasty risotto, of the canals, and mostly of Allessandro.

"Look at the moon, cara mia," he had told her with a last goodbye. "Look at the North Star and know that I am looking at them too. How can we be apart when we see the same things?"

The next morning, her first thought was to get word to Allessandro somehow. She tore a page from her sketchbook and quickly scribbled a note.

"Allessandro, cara mia, I am betrayed by Papa and remain at Windsor until I find a way home. I will find a way."

"I can post that for you, Margaret," Alice said, readying herself for work. "I know how to slip it into the diplomat pouch bound for Italy or find a traveler willing to take it." Alice raked her hair back and put on her cap. "King Henry has a wonderful post system all over England. When a ship leaves for Italy, the captain will take it."

Maddalena hesitated, thinking of the warning Lucy had given her not to trust Alice. "Are you sure?"

"Oh yes, dear." Alice nodded her head emphatically.

"It sounds like a strange way to send messages, but I've never sent one before."

"Remember I said I'd take care of you like a daughter? A mother wouldn't lie to her daughter."

Maybe not, but a father would.

Renewed by her anger, she folded her letter, sealed it with candle wax, and handed it to Alice.

More than ever before, Maddalena understood what the abbot had meant when he spoke of faith. Alice might not have been the best place to invest it, but she was all Maddalena had.

4

Cabot Falls, Vermont
Present Day

*W*hen Matthew, the last of her brood, took his seat in the Suburban, Sofia finally relaxed. All of her children were safely in her presence. She glanced at the rearview mirror as she drove home, keeping a wary watch for any dark vehicles that might be following them.

"Until this business with the stalker is settled," Sofia announced, "you're not to be alone. I'm instituting the buddy system." When the children were small, Sofia and Jim had made the kids couple up and watch out for each other. At the call of "Buddy up!" the kids would clasp hands with whichever sibling was closest. She could still picture them walking to the park, Vanessa and Wynter holding hands and skipping in front of Matthew and Luke, who had linked arms and were marching in step. She used to worry so much for their safety, and she guessed that would never change.

Sofia tried to convince herself that the phone call was a prank with bad timing. On the other end was some kid at home sick, bored and unsupervised. There was no telling how many people got the same call. And the dark SUV was really just one among any number of dark SUVs—a lost tourist, a family on the way to dinner, a mom on her way to a PTA meeting.

Back home, Vanessa groaned at the sight of the official envelope. She ripped it open, howled like a wounded dog, and shoved it into Sofia's hands. "The fine is seventy-five dollars! What are they thinking?"

Sofia assigned her the task of hemming solid orange poplin into tablecloths. At four dollars each and a dollar per napkin, she would soon earn the ticket money. She chose oak leaves and acorns stenciled on a cream background for the napkins. She could use them for years.

Vanessa was doing a neat job on them with straight, even seams. Sofia was glad that her daughter hadn't inherited her own two left thumbs when it came to needlecrafts.

She watched Vanessa with envy. All her teenage daughter had to worry about was paying for a traffic ticket. Meanwhile, Sofia had locked her children in the house and armed the alarm.

When Jim got home, he wasn't quick enough to the alarm panel, and the whole house screamed its discontent. The alarm company called and Sofia gave the password while Jim apologized and kissed her on the cheek. Sofia gave him mock scowl when she had to field a call from Pat Cooper to explain what all of the racket was about, but she really didn't mind. In fact, she was happy to know the alarm system was working.

The following afternoon, Sofia removed one of her homemade pumpkin cheesecakes from the freezer just as the doorbell rang. It was Julie Butler and Marla Dixon, the other two-thirds of the Pinot Painters. Sofia could hear Julie's infectious laugh all the way in the kitchen.

"Let us in," Julie called through the door. "It's chilly, and these things are heavy."

Sofia opened the door and Julie bustled past her with her easel and art supplies, leaving the scent of citrus and jasmine in her wake. Sofia's gaze followed her for a moment. Only Julie would wear hot pink with that wild, curly red hair of hers. On her it worked.

Marla stopped to give Sofia a chilled bottle of pinot and a one-armed hug. Then she followed Julie to the four-season room to set up her easel.

Julie's green eyes sparkled with mischief as she joined Sofia in the kitchen and watched as she uncorked the wine to breathe. Julie always seemed so comfortable in her stylish Anne Klein outfits. Her philosophy was to be just dressy enough to be stylish, but not so high fashion as to overwhelm her clients. She worked in a local public relations firm, where image was everything.

Sofia tugged self-consciously at her casual flannel shirt, mentally comparing the two of them and coming up way short.

Marla joined them at the counter. She wore gray tweed bootcut slacks and a deep purple cable-knit sweater. Marla and Julie had both come directly from work, which in Marla's case was the library. Reserved and thoughtful, she was a perfect contrast to bubbly Julie.

The three women met once a week, no matter what else was going on, to paint, sip pinot, and shed their concerns. Sofia looked forward to seeing them, although she was less enthusiastic about sharing her personal woes. She liked to enjoy her friends, not burden them.

The trio left the cheesecake to thaw and the wine to breathe and went to the four-season room. It had warmed enough so that the frost on the windows had turned to rivulets, partially obscuring the outdoor scene. The room quickly reeked of turpentine and oil paints.

"Does anyone else get depressed this time of year?" Julie asked. "It seems that the weather has turned so gray and gloomy."

Sofia rummaged through her box until she found the green paint tube. "It's not so bad. There's mouse gray, dove gray, stone gray, charcoal gray, concrete grays before and after it's dry. And then there's ivory white, pure white, smoky white and—"

Julie threw her head back and laughed. She wiggled her well-manicured fingers in the air so that the bright red flashed like flickering flames. "Okay, I get your point. You know subtlety is not my strong suit."

Fall and winter had their beauty, but it was the green of the quilt square that Sofia was drawn to. She mixed the green and brilliant white paint until it looked like the quilt square. She planned to add its embroidered leaf motif as an interesting background to a Renaissance scene.

The swatch intrigued her. Green was so different from everything she'd found in her research of the period, which made her wonder about its authenticity.

"Are you finding anything useful in the books you checked out?" Marla asked after peering over at Sofia's canvas.

Sofia nodded. "I discovered that Henry VIII was a lot different than I thought. I felt bad for him. Did you know his father actually referred to him as his 'spare king'? If his brother Arthur had lived, Henry never would have been king."

Julie squeezed some gray paint from a tube onto her palette. "Henry VIII? Isn't he the monster that beheaded a bunch of his wives?"

The word *monster* reverberated in Sofia's head. The sixteenth century had no monopoly on monsters, but she found it a lot easier to think about the one that lived five centuries ago than the one who was possibly stalking her daughter in a dark SUV.

"What's your family got to do with him?" Marla asked.

"I'm not exactly sure. But I hope to find out." *About both of them.* Only then would she feel her family was truly safe.

Windsor, England
Autumn 1532

Monsters haunted Maddalena's sleep, no doubt inspired by the real ones from this new life to which her father had exiled her. How could he leave her to the likes of Mabel Swan? How could he cast her away like a broken bisque figurine?

Maddalena stretched, trying to release the muscles that had tightened from the chill. She sat up to see Alice kneeling over an ornately carved chest that seemed very out of place in her small, humble quarters. Perhaps it spoke of happier times for the seamstress.

The lid creaked as if it had been a long time since it was last opened. Alice retrieved a gown, kirtle, and petticoat in unbleached linen, all neatly folded atop other clothes. "Here, Lily. Dress quickly and you will not feel the cold so much. They are all yours, a change for each day. The pretty blue one is for Sunday."

Lily? Maddalena nodded without speaking. She didn't correct Alice. Perhaps the clothes belonged to Lily, whoever she was. After she had changed, Alice handed her a dark wool cloak. "We must hurry if we want to break our fast before we leave."

Hens scattered as Alice led Maddalena across the yard and through the tavern's back door. The noise of night was gone, and the benches and tables held no evidence of the evening celebrations. Alice went over to the hearth and stirred the embers. Slowly they turned rosy and the flame licked at the logs. Maddalena pulled her cloak closer and stood by her.

Alice ladled a mixture of lamb and potatoes from the pot

that hung over the fire. It had cooled, but to an empty stomach it was welcome. When they finished, Alice wiped the bowls and returned them to the cabinet.

Maddalena and Alice hurried through town, up the hill to the palace grounds, and to the sewing room in Windsor Castle. They had no sooner settled on the bench with their sewing when a young woman appeared at the door and motioned for Mabel to come into the corridor. When Mabel returned, she looked flustered. "Margaret, you are to go with Lady Emma."

"Why?" Maddalena stood, crossing her arms defensively. "I've done nothing wrong. Where am I going?" Fear gripped her like fingers around her throat.

Mabel sniffed. "Do as you're told. And take your sketchbook with you. Don't speak unless you are told to do so. And observe etiquette."

In the hall, Maddalena found herself face-to-face with a girl no older than she. With her crimson brocade clothes and the gold brooch on a chain, she looked every bit the lady.

"What is happening? Should I be frightened?" Maddalena asked. Her heart beat rapidly, and she felt the blood rush through her temples.

Lady Emma walked briskly, and Maddalena fell in step with her.

"Don't be frightened," Lady Emma whispered. "This is a good thing, really. Queen Catherine asked me to fetch you."

"What?" Maddalena stopped short. "The queen? Why me?" Had the queen somehow heard of her plight? Perhaps she would send her home.

Lady Emma stopped and turned toward her. "I am only an attendant. I could not say. I can say only that whatever you have heard from those wags, Her Grace is very much still the queen. Now hurry. You must not keep her waiting."

She led Maddalena through an impressive area of the castle

to a heavily carved door with two guards. Inside, a pale, dark-eyed woman sat stiffly in a deeply tufted velvet chair that dwarfed her physically, yet she appeared in full command of the others hovering about her. A young woman dressed in indigo poured tea from a gold-leaf porcelain pot.

Lady Emma traipsed away as daintily as a dancer, leaving Maddalena standing in front of the Queen of England. Maddalena curtsied clumsily, remembering that she was not to rise until she had been given permission.

"Rise. Sit," Queen Catherine said and looked to one of the seated girls, nodding.

The girl rose, and Maddalena hesitantly took her place on the red velvet bench. The queen waved her hand like a butterfly wing, and the young women exited through a side door and closed it behind them.

Maddalena realized that she was now alone with the Queen of England. She could feel beads of perspiration gathering above her lip as the woman quietly studied her.

"You have brought your interpretations of the latest fashions, yes?" The queen's Spanish heritage was still detectable in her words, but just barely.

"Yes, Your Highness."

"May I see them, please?"

In her haste and nervousness, Maddalena knocked the book to the floor at the queen's feet. She quickly knelt to retrieve it. "Oh! I'm so sorry, I—"

Queen Catherine held her hand up to stop Maddalena's apology. She accepted the book in one hand and cupped Maddalena's chin in the other, lifting her face toward her. "Do not be afraid, child. You and I are not so different. You are not here of your own free will, but because of your father. And you are now called by an English name."

Maddalena's lip trembled, and she willed it to stop. Try as she might, she could not will the tears to vanish from her eyes.

"My name was once Catalina, so you see, I understand."

It was as if Maddalena truly saw the queen for the first time. The sadness in her eyes and the tired lines in her face touched her heart. It turned out that even a woman of the highest rank was no more privileged than the daughter of a merchant.

"I will request that for an hour each day, you come to my chambers as long as I remain here. You will teach us the embroidery designs you have brought."

"Oh, yes!" Maddalena realized that she had been too bold in shouting out her answer. She apologized. She liked the idea of being away from Mabel for an hour. But she was disturbed by the queen's words. "As long as I remain." She recalled that Lucy had said that the queen's days were numbered, and it seemed that the queen had confirmed this gossip.

"And now I request that you repair the hem of the gown I'm wearing. I seem to have caught my heel." Queen Catherine stood and slowly turned the pages of the sketchbook while Maddalena knelt to repair the hem.

She was on her knees stitching when the door to the apartment burst open. She was suddenly trapped between two people, one of them a male. The quality of his hose and shoes told her that he was extremely rich and high ranking, but she didn't dare look up.

"I have received word that the French and Austrian ambassadors will be here in time for the holidays," the man's voice announced. "It is important that England appears united and strong. I will expect your attendance at the celebrations. You will sit at the same table and make polite conversation, if it will not break your sour face to smile and laugh on occasion."

Maddalena was horrified. She fervently wished that she could shrink. Why didn't one of them dismiss her? Couldn't he see her right there at his feet? She had no doubt who it was.

"Will *she* be there?" Queen Catherine asked. Her voice was even and calm.

"No. At the end of the dinner, you will feign a headache and excuse yourself so that we may then enjoy the dancing and celebration."

"Yes, my lord. By then I doubt I will have to feign a headache. But I shall take my leave and pray for you and our country before retiring."

"I don't need your prayers. I need your consent. I need your signature on the documents."

"Never, my lord. I took an oath before God, until death. You took that same oath. Even if the pope allows it, which he will not, it is to God that I made my promise. I will not allow you to so easily dismiss our daughter and me. Mary shall not live in disgrace."

"You will not *allow*? You forget your place, woman."

Maddalena's hands shook so that she pricked her finger with the needle. She bit her lip to keep from crying out in pain.

"As you may remember, an annulment requires you to return the dowry that you have spent to impress other monarchs and your courtesan. What will you give up, Henry? Your extravagant pageants, perhaps? Your hunting trips? Your courtesan?"

"Bah!" The feet did an about-face and disappeared through the door, which banged loudly as it slammed shut.

Queen Catherine slumped back into the chair, her face expressionless. She seemed suddenly aware that Maddalena was still there and had witnessed it all. "Go. I will send for you tomorrow. Need I remind you that silence is not only golden but also wise?" She handed the sketchbook back to Maddalena with an amazingly steady hand.

Maddalena curtsied and turned to flee as several of the queen's ladies rushed in. Had they been listening, or was it the slam of the door that alerted them?

Until now, Maddalena had not thought of the sewing room as a refuge. As she ran away from the royal apartments, an old Italian saying came to mind: *È meglio che si dica 'qui il tale fuggi' che 'qui il tale mori.* "It is better to say 'here he ran' than 'here he died.'" She had worried before that she didn't know enough to survive her service at the castle. Now she worried that knowing too much could be just as dangerous. Had witnessing such an abomination made her even more vulnerable than before?

5

Sofia had never felt more vulnerable in her quaint village of Cabot Falls. The mysterious SUV and the phone warning had her on edge. She tried to shake it off; she needed to concentrate on her tasks.

A light mist fell on the windshield, and Sofia switched on the wipers, adjusting them to a slight delay between swipes. She hated the squeak they made with no moisture to push aside. It was like fingernails across a chalkboard, and she didn't need anything else to jar her already-frayed nerves.

Sofia patted her vest pocket to be sure she hadn't forgotten to bring her shopping list. Now if she'd only remember to read it. At the butcher's she ordered two turkeys for next month—one for the family and one for a catering job. She made a mental note to invite Marla and her son, Tim, who was Wynter's age. Marla had been a widow for over ten years now, but grief had a way of showing up unannounced on holidays.

As she approached the stop sign, Sofia glanced in her rearview mirror to be sure no one was following too closely on the slick street. She saw an SUV behind her, either blue-gray or charcoal or maybe even dark blue. She couldn't be sure; colors faded without the sun's help. The visor was down, covering the driver's eyes, and a dark woven scarf obscured the chin. Sofia couldn't even tell if the driver was male or female. Was that scarf to keep warm or to hide identification?

"There is no stalker," she told herself out loud, but she wasn't convinced. She pulled into the parking lot of Walker's Grocery, and the SUV continued on. She hadn't even realized that she was holding her breath. She let it out with a heavy sigh. "There is no stalker," she said again, feeling a little silly.

Sofia bought bags of fresh vegetables and fruits along with the specials of the day. After loading her bags into her vehicle, she returned the cart to the designated spot and slid behind the wheel. There was a flier stuck between the wet windshield and the wiper. She pulled it inside, crumpled it, and tossed it into her purse to throw away later.

Sofia backed out of her parking space and took note of the many dark SUVs in the parking lot. They were everywhere in Cabot Falls. With its rolling hills and nasty winters, cute little compacts wouldn't do.

As she drove home, she continued to scan the parking lots and roads for a mystery vehicle. Even though *she* hadn't seen a stalker, that didn't necessarily mean there wasn't one. Maybe he was only interested in following Vanessa. That thought chilled her to the core. No amount of convincing would ever quell her protective instincts when it came to her children.

Sofia spent the morning washing, cutting, and stowing her purchases in the fridge and freezer. By the time she'd finished, the mist had turned into a downpour. Fergus patted her leg with his paw and sat, offering her a paw shake.

"I didn't forget you. Here, good dog." She offered him a bone-shaped biscuit, which he carried to his favorite corner, then turned three times before settling with it. She decided to brew herself a cup of green tea to chase the damp chill away.

While the bag steeped, she remembered the flier she'd thrown into her purse. Sofia retrieved it and was about to throw it into the trash when something caught her attention. It wasn't a flier, but a handwritten note. The ink had run from the rain so most of it was unreadable. She smoothed the wrinkles and stared at the one still-legible word in bold block print: *DANGER!*

Trembling, Sofia reached for her cell phone. She realized that the police would probably think she was paranoid. Even if she told them about the SUV, what could they do?

Instead of dialing 911, she called her neighbor. After all, Pat had seen the suspicious SUV. She would understand. "Pat? I'll trade you a cup of tea for some advice."

Moments later, Pat Cooper pulled off her yellow slicker and left it on the covered stoop to drip. She wore a T-shirt with the face of the handsome gray-haired special agent from her favorite television show. She smiled when Sofia stepped back and took note of it. "I wear it because it makes Homer a little jealous."

Pat made herself comfortable at the kitchen table, and Sofia gave her a mug of tea. She quickly told Pat about Vanessa being followed and the note on her windshield. "I know it's not enough to go to the police with, but—"

Pat Cooper pulled out her notebook. "There was a dark SUV in your driveway today." She flipped through her notes and read them to Sofia. "At 9:45 a.m., the driver got out of the vehicle and walked to the side door."

"What did he look like?"

"He looked like an adult, not a teenager. But you can't tell these days."

It hadn't occurred to Sofia that it might be a teenager. She made a mental note to ask Vanessa if any of her friends drove a dark SUV—someone with an odd sense of humor.

"I called to him that you'd be back shortly, but he jumped in his vehicle and left without saying a word. It happened so fast that I didn't get his license plate number."

"If someone put the note on my windshield at the same time," Sofia said, "then who was here?"

Pat squeezed Sofia's hand and offered to call Ryan Quimby. She knew the young police officer well as he had been in the last English class she taught before retiring. Sofia had dealt with him previously and realized that he had a good head on his shoulders. She nodded her approval.

Pat dialed the police dispatch number. "This is Mrs. Cooper. Tell Officer Quimby to call me ASAP. It is important." She gave dispatch Sofia's number. "We'll get the perp." She winked at Sofia. "Homer hates it when I talk like that."

Sofia was grateful that Pat insisted on staying until Officer Quimby arrived. He jotted notes in a spiral-bound book that was only slightly bigger than Pat's. "I g-guess you ladies have both touched this flier." His face flushed, probably from embarrassment at the uncharacteristic stutter. Sofia could empathize with him. Their old teacher had that effect.

Pat immediately apologized. "A rookie mistake. I know better."

"The rain probably washed away the prints anyway," Quimby said.

"But the oils on our fingers would repel water, Ryan. You should take our prints for elimination," Pat said.

"Uh, y-yes ma'am," the officer mumbled. "I'll get the kit from the car."

"The black-and-white," Pat corrected.

"Yes ma'am."

Poor guy. Sofia lifted her teacup to her lips to keep from laughing. The process of giving her fingerprints sobered her quickly enough. It was not only Vanessa in danger. It was the entire Parker family. But why?

Windsor, England
Autumn 1532

"Why do we have to go on such an ugly day, Alice?" Maddalena complained. "It's so cold."

Even the heartiest weeds had turned to brittle straw, and the sky was a solid sheet of mouse gray. Alice called it "pea soup." It hurt Maddalena's artistic soul to live in this colorless world.

Town wags reminded anyone who would listen that it was the coldest year they could remember. The unexpected snowfall had turned to an icy rain that dripped from the eaves, settled into wagon ruts, and displaced earth where it pooled.

On rare occasions, the Venice Lagoon froze, briefly trapping the merchant ships. But never had Maddalena experienced the depth of cold that now penetrated her body and chilled her bones.

Smoke curled from the chimneys, creating a heavy fog that ringed the palace and other buildings in the courtyard. It was as if the guard towers had vanished. Thunder rumbled in the distance. "God is moving his furniture," her mother had once told her when Maddalena had run fearfully to her, burying her face in the soft folds of her mother's dress. Maddalena pushed it from her thoughts as her foot slipped in the mud and she flailed her arms to keep her balance.

Rains came almost daily now. Even when it didn't rain, the air was damp, and the opaque mist blotted out the sun. The path was devoid of other pedestrians. Windsor looked as oppressive to her now as it had when first she saw it. She might live there now, displaced and a castaway, but she refused to call it home.

She left a path of dripping water as she climbed the stone steps and hurried down the hall to the sewing room. Her clothes clung heavily to her as she stood with Alice in front of the hearth, watching its crimson flames lick the logs and shoot out sparks from the oozing sap. Maddalena gradually rotated her body to let the heat dry her cap and clothes and warm her skin.

She massaged her fingers. It was as if a thousand pins were jabbing her hands until gradually she could wiggle them. The room reflected a golden glow from the beeswax candles that lined the windowsills. Sewing could not stop because the light was poor.

Despite slow travels, the guests and their entourages arrived daily. Preparations were well underway for the Christmas celebrations. Guest areas smelled like spices and citrus. Hearths bore pine boughs and Venetian glass balls and bows of silk, a stark contrast to the outdoors and the servants' areas. Maddalena imagined the festivities at her home—everyone dressed in their finest, goblets clinking, and platters of delicate treats being passed around.

The king's royal artist, Hans Holbein the Younger, was nearly finished with a mural that spanned one wall of the great hall where festivities would take place. Maddalena sneaked a peek every morning, drawn there by the familiar aroma of turpentine, the artists' perfume. She could close her eyes and, for a brief moment, be on the dock, painting at Allessandro's side. She made a mark in her book for another day she had been abandoned to the king's service, six marks and a slash to mark each week. As the weeks passed, her anxiety grew. She hadn't much expected to hear from Papa. But why had she not heard from Allessandro? Had he received her notes?

Still shaken from witnessing the monarchs' encounter, she was determined to make the queen's dress more beautiful than anyone else's. The fashion trend was to slash the outer garment to reveal the rich lining. Instead of horizontal slashes, she cut star shapes to reveal the white silk lining. She hoped that the queen would approve. If not, she'd have to work through the night to have the sleeves ready for the pageant and dinner.

Maddalena jumped at the sound of her English name. She looked up from her work as Lucy spoke to her. "Well, Margaret, what was it like? Tell us, Mistress 'igh-and-Mighty. You didn't speak of it at all when you returned yesterday. Did you really see the queen's apartments? We want to know everything."

Maddalena picked up a royal blue coat. She pinned silver lace a thumb's width from the hemmed edge as she spoke. "You mean *you* want to know everything. It was nice."

"Nice? Is that all you got to say—*nice*? None of us 'as ever laid eyes on it," Lucy persisted, "much less, seen 'er at more than a distance. Is she as old as they say?"

Maddalena bristled, recalling Queen Catherine's kindness to her and the depth of the sadness on her face. "It's pretty, I guess. There's a good deal of red velvet and brocade. Gold and silver and fur are everywhere. And the queen is lovely and kind."

The encounter still echoed in her mind. She had observed dignity and calm under extreme circumstances. It brought up long-forgotten words, angry words from her childhood that invaded her sleep and sat heavily in her consciousness even now. The voices in her head—were they those of the king and queen? Or were they her mother and father? Images flashed in her mind like lightning and disappeared just as quickly. She pushed them back into her memory vault and slammed the door on them. *They are best forgotten.* Maddalena wanted to emulate the queen's strength.

"The queen had best enjoy 'erself whilst she can, is all I'm saying," Lucy said. "If the king can get his annulment and marry Lady Anne and she gives him a son, Queen Catherine, her daughter, and the young duke will be a head shorter."

"Lucy, your tongue will get you hanged one of these days. You best use that needle to sew your mouth shut," Mabel told her.

Lucy threw her head back in the loud cackle that Maddalena found so irritating.

Preparations for the celebration kept all floors of the castle busy as acrobats, mummers, and jugglers rehearsed.

The evening of the pageant, Christmas Eve, the hall was bright and cheery. The crystal chandeliers and strategically placed mirrors reflected and multiplied the flames of the candles.

The entire court, including the mummers, wore costumes of royal blue and white, and the guests laughed and applauded and danced into the night. Maddalena, Rose, and Lucy were assigned serving duties so that each guest had a personal servant standing behind them at the table, ready to fill their goblets from wine decanters and refill their silver plates or remove them.

Maddalena could see King Henry with the queen. He looked solicitous and cheerful. He presented a front of marital bliss and cooperation that impressed upon the guests the image of a kingdom standing strong and united. At the end of the meal, as if on cue, the queen excused herself and swept from the hall, followed by her attendants like partridge chicks following their mother. There was no hint in her expression that this was a command performance.

While the guests were viewing the pageant, Maddalena hurried to the kitchen with an empty goblet—and straight into the arms of Rose's beloved Thom Bell. Tall and thin with a pockmarked face, he reminded Maddalena of a hungry cat on the prowl.

"'Allo there, li'l bird," he said. "What 'ave we 'ere?"

"Let go of my arm!" Maddalena protested.

"Just a li'l kiss, and I'll let ye pass."

"Get away from me. You are vile."

"Vile, is it? What's that supposed to mean, li'l bird?" He

grasped the cross that hung around her neck. "What's this? A seamstress with such a fine piece of gold? You won't mind me taking it now, will you?"

The kitchen was massive, and servants bustled about, scouring pots and washing the plates and goblets as they were returned. A ruddy-faced man who had been barking orders at them all night looked up from the stack of plates and frowned but made no move to stop the young man.

"I'll tell Rose," Maddalena said. She pushed him, and the goblet fell to the floor and shattered on the stone. She covered a gasp with her hand.

"Aw, I know who you are now. You be the one Rose calls 'Mistress 'igh-and-Mighty.' I 'ave a better place for this crucifix. It could fetch me something a bit more practical." He yanked at the cross and the fragile chain broke.

"That's mine!" Maddalena yelled. She snatched it back as he tried to tuck it inside his tunic. In their struggle, several sterling spoons spilled from his tunic and clattered to the floor.

One of the cooks motioned to several men, and they pulled Thom away.

Maddalena could think only of Rose at that moment. "Where are they taking him?"

"He won't be stealing or bothering you again—ever," the cook told her.

"I have my necklace back."

"And the king has his spoons. But no one steals from the king and lives. He'll hang for sure."

"No, please! What will I tell—"

"Where are they taking Thom? What's going on?" Rose stood staring at them, her eyes a mix of fear and fire. She balled her fist and would have struck Maddalena had two of the kitchen help not restrained her. "You!"

"Rose, I . . ." Maddalena shrugged helplessly. "Rose, he's a thief. He—"

"Don't you say anything about my Thom. I will get you for this."

Maddalena had glimpsed the knife Rose wore strapped at her ankle. She had no doubt that the girl would be willing to use it.

6

Cabot Falls, Vermont
Present Day

"*I* could use some inspiration right now," Sofia told her son Matthew. She leaned over the counter as she sketched different designs for the cake she was supposed to donate to the cakewalk. None of them seemed right. "The chairwoman said that they would put my cake in the silent auction instead of selling it in slices. She wants at least seventy-five dollars for it, so it has to be spectacular and showy!"

Matthew stood with the refrigerator door open, staring into it. "Make it big."

"Get an apple and close the door," Sofia told him. "Tell me, what do you think of when you think of Halloween?"

He grabbed a Red Delicious and took a bite before answering. "Ninjas." He wiped juice from his chin with the sleeve of his sweater.

"Sleeves are not napkins, Matthew. Use a paper towel. What besides ninjas? I mean traditional Halloween."

"Oh, then I like giant spiders with fuzzy legs and bug eyes and bats. But no pumpkins. Definitely no pumpkins."

Sofia scratched out the pumpkin cake design she had drawn on the page.

"Are you sure no ninjas? I want to be a ninja for Halloween."

As Matthew talked, Sofia drew a hairy spider with long legs.

"Can I go trick-or-treating somewhere besides our cul-de-sac this year, please?"

Her spider turned into a dark SUV before her eyes. She blinked the image away.

Matthew tilted his head to see what Sofia had drawn and nodded in approval as he chewed another bite of his apple. "That's good," Matthew said. "Maybe some zombies too."

Sofia nodded, agreeing that zombies might be easier to do than skeletons. She drew a pale green figure atop the spider. "Like this?"

"Yeah! But you need more junk, Mom. People want lots of things for their money."

Jim got home a little later than normal. He tutored after school and stopped off to deposit the check on Fridays. He removed his backpack and jacket and hung them on the peg labeled Dad. "I just saw a patrol car circle the cul-de-sac."

"It's a long story that can wait until after supper," Sofia said, planting a kiss on his lips. He tasted like peppermint candy, which explained the slight red tinge at the corner of his mouth. "We're all inside now, Jim. Will you please set the alarm?"

She transferred the pot roast to the platter and arranged the red potatoes and carrots around it. Friday night was traditionally pot roast and "kitchen conference" afterward. Jim doled out allowances, guaranteeing perfect attendance. And it gave everyone an opportunity to receive praise or express concerns and remind one another of important dates.

"Do any of you have suggestions about the booth for the carnival?" Sofia asked. "I'd like to have something that fits the Renaissance Festival too. Maybe something we could use all year."

Luke spoke up. "Dad, can't we make something that we can break down and put up with bolts? That way it can stow in the garage when Mom doesn't need it."

"Good idea. We can definitely do that," Jim said. "What's wrong with using an Old English theme for Halloween too? That way we don't have to repaint it after Renaissance."

"Did they have ninjas in reno sauce?" Matthew asked.

"It's *Renaissance*, ninja boy," Vanessa teased. "Like a long time ago, with kings and queens and knights and stuff like that."

"And don't forget jesters—like you, Matthew," Luke said.

"What kind of gesture? You mean like this?" Matthew made a few karate chops in the air, getting a laugh from the whole table.

"*Jester*, not *gesture*," Luke said. "It's kind of like a clown."

Matthew shrugged. "I can live with that." Matthew made more karate chops while the other kids laughed and shouted out other gestures for him to do.

"I think this meeting's adjourned," Jim said.

"I'll post help wanted lists on the bulletin board by Monday," Sofia said above the chatter. "Volunteer unless you want to be drafted."

After the younger Parkers left to watch a movie, Sofia told Jim about the note on the windshield.

Jim stared at her in stunned silence. "Why didn't you bring that up at the meeting, Sofia? The kids need to know what's going on. Did Officer Quimby say what the police could do?"

"He put us on drive-by, just in case it's not a prank," she said.

"What can *we* do? I think the kids should carry pepper spray," Jim suggested.

Sofia wrapped her arms around his waist. "I'm not trying to keep it from them. But there's a big difference in understanding for a seventeen-year-old girl and a ten-year-old boy. We should talk to them individually. Truthfully, I'm relieved that this isn't about someone obsessed with Vanessa. Still, I can't think of anyone that we might have offended. Can you?"

"It has to be a prank, doesn't it?" Jim rubbed the stubble that was starting to shadow his jawline. "But why us?"

Light reflected from the gold-framed mirror opposite the window, and Sofia crossed the room to peer out. It was the patrol car again. It gave her a sense of safety to know that they were on the drive-by list, at least for now.

But Jim was right. Why them? It was scary to think that they might know someone who bore such ill will toward them. She wondered what the unreadable part of the note had said. Perhaps the word *danger* had said it all. It was a threat she took seriously.

Windsor, England
Winter 1532

"I take Rose's threat seriously," Maddalena told the Venetian ambassador's secretary, a nervous young man with a constantly shifting gaze. "I believe that my life is in danger if I remain here." She realized that she would have no chance to speak with the ambassador himself, who was at Windsor for the Christmas and New Year activities.

The secretary blinked but said nothing. He looked furtively around the room.

"If you will only secure my passage with your entourage," she pleaded.

He shrugged helplessly. "There is nothing I can do."

"A message, then? Will you carry a letter? Please." She shoved a sealed note into his hand before he could protest.

"I'll carry it as far as the government house. Beyond that I promise nothing."

Alice was angry when she told her about the exchange. "You

must never do that again," she warned Maddalena. "You may not be native-born, but you are not immune to punishment. You must never approach the king's guests like that."

"It was only his employee," Maddalena defended. "Alice, none of the letters you passed to the outside have been answered. I don't know if any of them have reached Allessandro."

"He probably chose not to answer them. He has accepted that you are here to stay. But don't worry, Lily. I will take care of you always."

Maddalena drew back when Alice tried to hug her. *Always?* Did Alice truly believe that she would stay forever? "Alice, I'm not ungrateful, but I don't belong here. I am not Lily. Was Lily your daughter?" She paused. "Where is she, Alice?"

Alice busied herself and pretended not to hear the question.

Maddalena continued to wonder about Lily. Had she worn those clothes? Had she died? Or did she run away from a smothering life?

The end of the 1532 brought new challenges to the royal household and to the seamstresses in turn. Word leaked from the royal chambers and quickly spread through the castle corridors that the king would have a visitor in the spring. King Francis, the French monarch, would make a state visit to see him.

King Henry sent diplomats—ostensibly spies—to the French king's court. To his dismay, they returned affirming that the rumors were true—Francis was handsome, a dashing monarch who rivaled King Henry with his fashion sense and knightly skills. They reported that the French king was not only a fine figure of a man, but he also wore a beautiful, thick beard.

At six feet two inches and with outstanding ginger hair, King Henry was an imposing monarch in his own right. His sense of fashion was widely accepted as the best, thanks in no small part to the seamstresses and his lavish spending. Until now, however, he had been clean-shaven.

Now King Henry set out immediately to grow a beard that would not just rival that of King Francis, but with its golden-red hue, surpass it. He was concerned about the wardrobe too, especially the first impression. He summoned Maddalena.

"M-m . . . me?" she asked when a page appeared in the sewing room with a summons from King Henry himself. Her instinct was to run and never stop. She was aware that this was the proverbial double-edged sword. Her favor with the monarchs created hostility in the sewing room, especially with Mabel. Worse, it offered an opportunity to fall from favor if she failed the king. Anonymity was so much safer. Alas, that time had passed, and Maddalena would have to do her best under pressure.

Apprehension stole her voice as she curtsied before the king and waited for him to tell her to rise. What if he remembered her from the queen's chambers?

"Rise," he said finally. "You are the one who created the stars on the queen's dress?"

She stared dumbly and nodded.

"You show imagination," he said. "You will use it to create a wardrobe for the court that will show that pompous Frenchman what the English court looks like. It must be extraordinary. It would be unfortunate if we appeared similar, understand? No ordinary red or blue or purple. Nothing expected. We must stop him in his tracks."

Maddalena nodded.

"Is the girl a mute?" he asked the page.

"N-n-no, Your Highness," she said before the page could answer. "I'm Venetian."

King Henry threw his head back and laughed. "Venetian! So you are!"

Maddalena didn't like being laughed at, especially when she didn't understand why. "I-I wasn't sure I was supposed to speak, or how to address you, Sire."

"Address me with respect, young Venetian. Now, what will shock the boots off the French frog? We don't have much time before spring. We will hunt and have tournaments and feasts."

Maddalena forgot that she was speaking to the most powerful monarch, and momentarily she treated him like a co-conspirator. "Green, Your Majesty."

"Green, like castle messengers? Explain yourself."

"King Francis will most probably keep to the traditions—dark red, royal purple, indigo." She had heard whispers of King Henry's vanity. "In the fabric vault is a pale green silk. It is nothing like the messengers' harsh green. It is refined and exquisite. It would be not only a symbol of spring—of youth—but it would show your glorious hair and magnificent beard to the best advantage."

It was as if time halted as he mulled her suggestion. "Green." He rolled the word like a slow growl, but Maddalena could see that he was visualizing himself in the color.

"It is the green of new growth on the trees," she said to help him visualize. "It speaks of promise and potential, of hope and—and good things to come." And then it hit her. What if she was wrong?

Maddalena suggested that she complete an ensemble so that he might judge for himself. She promised it in three days. With the five of them working ten hours a day, she thought they could produce a proper garment that would convey everything she believed he wanted. It was not the time to bargain with him. But perhaps if he was pleased, she could request passage home. It was worth a try.

Would she have the full cooperation of the seamstresses? Rose hated her, but did she hate her enough to fail the king? And Lucy—would she stir up trouble just to amuse herself? No, Mabel would see to it that they worked hard.

When she was dismissed, Maddalena broke into a brisk shuffle, dashed into the stairwell, and stopped short of running into the boy with the ginger hair.

"Mad Margaret!" he teased. "We meet once more. You dash about the palace like a wild mare." He grinned impishly.

"I've no time for idle chat," she replied. "And you best pick up your pace too. There's work to be done." She stepped around him and down the stone steps as she spoke.

"And what should I be doing, Mad Margaret?" he called down after her. His voice bounced off the walls, sounding hollow.

"Whatever you usually do, only better and faster," she called back before letting the door to the stairwell shut behind her. She couldn't help but wonder about that boy. She sometimes saw him in the courtyard in mock sword fights and wrestling, a gang of rowdy boys circled around him. And then time would pass with no sightings at all.

When she arrived back in the sewing room, Maddalena was acutely aware that her sudden attention by the throne made Mabel resentful and suspicious and even fearful that she might lose her position as head seamstress. She realized that her best chance was to make her an ally, not an enemy. How she approached Mabel would make all the difference in her success.

She asked to see the older woman in the fabric vault. "The king trusts you to guide us through a special garment for his approval," Maddalena said. "I am to be your liaison so that you may devote your valuable time to the project."

That seemed to be the right approach, as Mabel nodded and seemed less guarded as Maddalena continued. She explained the festivities scheduled for spring. "It is in this pale green silk with this deeper green brocaded velvet that his message of strength, youth, and potential will echo with every member of his court. It must all be done in secret."

Secrecy appealed to the seamstresses, and for the three days each worked diligently on her part. On the third day, they pieced their work together into the single garment. Mabel sent word to the king's chamberlain that it was ready for his opinion. Although Maddalena left the gown plain, she cut a square of the silk and embroidered scattered olive leaves on it. She suggested that creating a set of sleeves with the design would make an interesting contrast and would set his wardrobe apart from the others'.

In his chambers for the fitting, King Henry walked out from behind the screen and Maddalena gasped. He was even more imposing that she had imagined he would be. His beard in only three days had become impressive with his golden-red hair. She could not imagine the French king even coming close to such elegance.

It was decided. The entire court would wear green to greet King Francis. Henry called his best pageant and festival planners together and plotted a welcome that would once and for all show the Frenchman who was the superior monarch.

As Maddalena and the others worked furiously on the court's wardrobe, spies returned with their reports. The French king was bringing a hundred servants. King Henry commanded 150 servants be ready to travel. He decided to meet King Francis on the road, a day away from Windsor. There they would have the tournaments, hunting parties, and feasts. It would give the servants left behind more time to make Windsor magnificent for the formal activities.

When the French caravan was two days away, the English caravan left Windsor. The royals and nobles rode in matching black carriages. Most of the servants, including Maddalena, walked.

By then the roads had been smoothed of winter's ruts, and fresh leaves adorned the trees. They set up the royal tents, installed a stage, and prepared for hunting and the tournaments.

King Henry's spies reported that King Francis's caravan was less than an hour away, setting off a flurry of last-minute activity. The stable boys brought forward several dozen matching ebony jennets with glistening black leather and silver saddles.

The ladies and nobles mounted their horses on the king's command. He mounted his own black jennet standing in the center of the road, where the sun cast dappled light through the trees. Tall in the saddle, with his golden crown blending almost completely with his hair, King Henry was an imposing figure.

Maddalena heard the stamp of hooves as the French king's caravan came around the stand of trees and to a complete halt. The king, his head wearing no crown, was attired in traveling clothes and was drenched in perspiration. He looked stunned as King Henry cued his horse forward to hail his rival.

King Henry had accomplished his first goal. If the remainder of the outdoor portion of entertainment went as well, Maddalena believed she would have a chance to leave with his blessing. She dared not think what could go wrong.

7

Cabot Falls, Vermont
Present Day

*E*verything that could go wrong did. Sofia was trying unsuccessfully to balance an egg-shaped piece of cake on licorice strips that looked like spider legs when she realized it was time to take Wynter to speech therapy. Her younger daughter had made great progress since getting the cochlear implant, but she still felt awkward in conversations.

In the car, Wynter surprised Sofia when she said that Doug Sanders had invited her to the Harvest Ball at the school—her first real date.

"Doug Sanders?" Sofia asked. "Isn't he the very same boy who's brought on a flood of tears from you for the past month? You said he was mean and he picked on you."

"Yes, but Vanessa said that he was probably shy too. He was picking on me because he liked me, and he didn't know how to tell me. She said girls are more mature, and sometimes we have to help boys figure things out."

Sofia had forgotten how awkward teenage courting was. "So, how did you work it out?"

"I walked up to him in the lunch line and said, 'Doug Sanders, if you like me you'll take me to the dance.'"

Sofia burst out laughing. "The subtle approach, huh? How did he react?"

Wynter smiled. "He dropped his food tray and then asked me to the dance. It's okay, isn't it, Mom? I mean, I'm almost sixteen."

"I'll call his parents. I imagine they will agree to drive you. I'll offer to pick up both of you afterward. We will need to think about a dress." Sofia pulled to a stop in front of the speech therapy clinic. "After your appointment, do not come outside until you see me. Got it?"

As happy as she was for her youngest daughter, this added one more strain on the budget and her time. Maybe it was time to call on the Super-Aunts. Back home, Sofia dialed Aunt Louisa first and poured out her woes about the need for social and holiday clothes—the Renaissance Festival, the Halloween Carnival, and the dance.

As expected, Aunt Louisa said that she and Aunt Rachel would come up with something. "I already have an idea percolating in my head. I'll call you tomorrow, all right?"

The next morning, Aunt Louisa called. "If we do some royal-looking outfits, they should work for Halloween too. Rachel thought how to adapt the girls' costumes for the dance so nobody would even suspect. I'm sure I'd have thought of it myself if she hadn't." Sofia's two aunts were in their sixties, but they had never given up their sibling rivalry. "The two of us have enough fabric leftover from family weddings to clothe a village. You know, the men wore skirts and tights back then. Do you think the boys will balk at tights?"

Sofia winced. "I can guarantee it, Aunt Louisa." That settled, she told her aunt about researching the reign of Henry VIII. "I'll email photos of some of their clothes from that era. I'll send you the measurements too. *Grazie mille,* Aunt Louisa. *Ciao.*"

Once wardrobe was being handled, Sofia could concentrate on what to serve at the bridal shower luncheon, the Renaissance Festival, and the Halloween Carnival. She spent the morning mixing the batter and baking six round layers to freeze until the day of the school carnival. She had just finished when Marla called.

"I located a biography of Elizabeth Blount, the mother of King Henry VIII's illegitimate son, Henry Fitzroy. It was written by one of her direct descendants, and it's in a bookstore in Brighton, England. I can't justify the expense for the library since it is so specific. It costs over thirty dollars."

"Ouch. That's steep right now," Sofia told her.

"If you'll agree to donate it when you're done, we can split the cost. The guy couldn't find any mention of your family names, but he said it included a lot of documents, the Tudor family tree, and information about life in the castle. You might be able to at least verify some of the things mentioned in the diary."

"It's a deal! Thank you, my friend." Sofia wanted to do a good job on the research, and if this book was as informative as her friend thought, it would be a good investment. She was so curious about the green fabric swatch. She couldn't avoid researching it any more than she could forget that someone, perhaps even someone she considered a friend, disliked her family enough to threaten them.

Every painting she had found so far showed the people in deep red or purple clothes. She was afraid that the green silk could be a fake, which would throw doubt on the integrity of the diary and the quilt itself. If only she could find an authentic painting of the monarchy or royals wearing green . . .

The Outskirts of Windsor, England
Spring 1533

Everywhere Maddalena looked, she saw the bright, fresh, green leaves. She basked in the sights and smells of spring in the forest,

away from Windsor—the gentle burbling of a nearby spring, a
butterfly in flight, and the amazing bright red of a little bird that
shrieked in protest when she startled it on the trail. She sketched
the creatures, the horses, and the people with such a marvelous
array of noses, mouths, eyes, and expressions.

They were all part of the same creation, yet so different. It
fascinated the artist in her. After being confined to a stuffy room
all winter, Maddalena felt a burst of renewed energy that made
her want to run, skip, and leap like a child.

The forest rang with cheers over the tournament games
that must have surely scared off all but the peskiest animals.
Only the squirrels intent on building their nests remained,
voicing their displeasure with high-pitched barks and throaty
growls. If the merry invaders regarded them at all, it was with
a passing fancy.

Maddalena had far less to do than she had imagined—no
more than mending hems snagged on a thorny bush or a knight's
tunic ripped during a show of strength while wrestling, fencing,
and jousting.

The feasts had gone on for three days when Maddalena heard
a loud commotion. The forest surrounding them was suddenly
alive with men carrying bows and wearing leather quivers of
arrows strapped to their backs. One of them approached the stage
where the royals sat watching the games. King Henry motioned
his soldiers to stand down.

"Outlaws," Lucy whispered. For once she seemed at a loss
for words.

"Outlaws?" Maddalena asked. "As in criminals?"

"More like people who prefer to live away from towns and
cities and rules—outside the reach of the law. I hear they are very
skilled and survive on what they have out here. The Hood family
and their friends have lived like this for generations."

The apparent leader bowed and spoke to King Henry. He challenged the king's knights to a contest, and King Henry accepted on their behalf. They spent the greater part of the day challenging one another and feasting—French, English, and the outlaws of the forest.

The leader, the one called Robin, invited Kings Henry and Francis to see where and how they lived and to eat a meal with them. Maddalena wasn't surprised when King Henry accepted with enthusiasm. He had been reveling in the wild turn of events.

Most of the nobles and servants to both kings seemed at a loss about what to do, so they milled about, mumbling to one another. Maddalena and Lucy followed on foot. "Until someone tells us not to, why should we not?" Maddalena asked.

They hadn't traveled the path even a half hour when they came to a clearing and halted. Suddenly more people appeared—women and children dressed in earthen colors that blended perfectly with the forest. Nearly hidden among the trees were primitive houses of logs with straw roofs and windows of oiled parchment.

The outlaw families shared their meal of roast wild pig, dandelion greens, and root vegetables. Maddalena witnessed a different King Henry. The tension and competitiveness had drained from him. He appeared relaxed and happy far away from the turmoil that awaited them at Windsor. The excursion opened Maddalena's eyes to the other Henry, a side of him she hoped she would be able to reach as she sought his help to leave. But she realized that his permission would not be enough. She had no resources except what others would allow.

Maddalena could not help but admire the outlaw families, despite their lives of privation, because they were freer than anyone. She saw herself more clearly. She realized that if she returned before she reached her majority, she would find herself back under her father's thumb. He would prevent her from achieving the things she wanted for her life—to be with Allessandro and to paint. At home she would be no freer than she was at Windsor, doing the will of the king, Mabel, and even Alice, whom she obeyed out of gratitude and a bit of fear.

Alice had given her shelter and food. In exchange, Maddalena had accepted her role as an obedient and protected daughter. She had quietly stood by while Alice introduced her to the innkeeper as her long-lost daughter who'd finally returned home. She had looked into the eyes of the others and seen pity, but she wondered if it was for Alice or for her.

Now Maddalena knelt by the spring and scooped up water, bathing her face. The ripples rolled outward and vanished, leaving only her reflection in the smooth water.

She could see that she was changing, her face narrowing, and her features a bit older. She looked more like her mother than she had when she left home. But she didn't want to be her mother, too weak to protect herself or her own daughter, her flesh and blood. "Who are you?" she asked her reflection.

"More important, who do you want to be?" a familiar voice asked.

Startled, she nearly tumbled headfirst into the spring. If the ginger-haired boy hadn't grabbed her shoulders, she might have.

"Good question," she said, pushing his hands away. "One thing I know I am not is Mad Margaret, so don't call me that. I am Maddalena Vitari. If I ever discover who that is, I'll let you know." She stumbled past him and down the path toward the boisterous noise of King Henry's camp.

The royal families had resumed their places on the platform. One of the queen's attendants presented a winner with a crown of wildflowers.

"Where's my son?" King Henry called out. "He challenges your best to a wrestling match. Where is the Duke of Richmond?"

"Here, Your Grace."

Maddalena felt the life drain from her as the ginger-haired boy stepped forward and bowed. *The king's son?* She had treated the *king's son* like an annoying gnat to be swatted away? Legitimate or not, he commanded influence. Given all the rules about heirs to the throne, he was the closest to the throne, even above his half-sister, Mary. Maddalena was torn between fear and anger that he had toyed with her on so many occasions.

She looked up as the duke slid one foot behind the bigger, older contestant and sent him crashing onto his back to the ground, then landed on top of him. The crowd cheered, and giggling ladies-in-waiting rushed to offer their handkerchiefs to the king's son. Declining, he trudged past Maddalena toward the spring, winking at her as he passed.

Lucy giggled. "He's beautiful, ain't he? He's much more popular with the common folks than his dad or his mum. Someday he'll throw his ol' man off, I say."

Maddalena looked around to be sure no one was close enough to hear. "Hush, Lucy. You will be hanged and take me with you."

Lucy threw her head back in a typical cackle, and Maddalena couldn't help but see how vulnerable the woman's neck was at that very moment. But her attention was drawn back to the crowd as King Henry, obviously buoyed not only by the duke's victory but also the renewed vigor he felt after the encounter with the outlaws, challenged King Francis to a contest. "Choose your game," he said.

"Jousting," the Frenchman countered. The two donned armor and were helped onto their equally protected horses at far ends of the gaming field, one on each side of the cloth barrier.

Maddalena closed her eyes and didn't open them until she heard screams. Although Francis had not yet reached him, King Henry was down, pinned beneath his fallen horse. "What happened?" she asked.

Nobles rushed to remove armor from the horse so that it could regain its feet. With the animal removed from the scene, it was quickly obvious that King Henry's leg had been cut by the armor meant to protect him. His physician knelt beside him.

Four men carried the king to his tent, and the rest of the court huddled nearby. The physician exited later, saying that the king would rest there until morning, when the festivities would be transferred to Windsor, where he could entertain more comfortably.

The caravan, now doubled in size with the addition of King Francis's entourage, made slow progress back the next day. Anxiety circulated in the royal carriages and seeped back to the supply wagons where the weary servants now occupied any space possible.

Rumors varied, from the king's demise from his wound to a possible overthrow of the crown, with the young duke, his older sister Mary, or even King Francis laying claim to it.

King Henry dispelled the rumors by walking into the palace alone, although the slight limp and pained expression on his face indicated it was a great effort to do so.

Maddalena and Lucy reported to the sewing room, unprepared for the onslaught of questions that greeted them. Lucy repeated her theory on the assent to the throne.

Maddalena took a practical approach. "The king's leg is extremely swollen, and the cut appears deep and painful. Mabel, is it possible for us to prepare hose that would ease his pain and disguise his wound? He seems determined to continue his entertainment as planned."

People were anxious, and gossip ran rampant. It seemed a dangerous time. Rumors said that Queen Catherine had been exiled once again. Others said that she was confined to her apartment under guard. Wherever the queen was, it was Lady Anne Boleyn who now sat at the king's side during all of the entertainments.

Some said it was because she spoke fluent French. Others gossiped that she was merely "jumping the flag," a reference to contest participants who began before the signal.

In this case, Anne was acting as queen while the true queen remained hidden away, and not by her choice. Maddalena thought that King Henry must have felt confident in his position of power compared with the young and inexperienced Frenchman to no longer pretend England was a united and happy country.

All of this was spoken in guarded whispers among the nobles, although surely the young French king heard all of it. King Henry dared not look weak, or the ambitious young monarch might decide to challenge England. That would be a big mistake and costly to them both.

Maddalena knew this was not the time to request her leave, especially when she had no idea of what she would find when she returned to Venice. Had Allessandro, like her father, simply forgotten about her?

8

Cabot Falls, Vermont
Present Day

$\mathcal{S}$ofia had forgotten about Robin Hood until she saw him mentioned in the quilt diary. While the vegetable stock simmered, she reread the segment. She'd always assumed he was a fictional character. That Maddalena Vitari had somehow wound up in Windsor Castle where Henry VIII held court had seemed suspect. Add to that incongruous mentions of the outlaw, and it seemed almost laughable.

She couldn't get the visual out of her head of some dashing film actor hiding behind trees with his bow and arrow. *You have to keep a sense of humor to keep a serious family history interesting,* she supposed. Yet the biography of Elizabeth Blount that Marla found quoted the ambassador from Italy in his report of the events surrounding the visit by King Francis. He described Hood as one of a long line of kinsmen by that name. They were not at all like the Hollywood version, but simply commoners who lived in the woods, much as modern survivalists do.

The phone rang, and it was Aunt Louisa with good news. She and Aunt Rachel were accomplishing much with the costumes. In particular, the ball dresses for the girls were turning out just as planned. They would adapt perfectly for the school dance, and no one would know the difference.

Sofia thought that it would probably take a Julie-style sales job to convince the girls that they would not be laughingstocks, but the budget was already strained. The most she could offer them were some dance-worthy shoes from the discount shoe store. If her little Cinderellas wanted to go to the ball, then they'd have to accept what their fairy god-aunts designed for them.

The timer on the range sounded, and Sofia turned off the flame and moved the soup pot near the sink. She drained the stock into containers and set the vegetables aside, minus the onions, to add to Fergus's meal. The nutrients were mostly in the stock, but he would enjoy the taste variety. She could use the stock in a few days for the pumpkin soup for what she now referred to as "the scary bridal luncheon." Gretchen had called yesterday to add one more to the count—the bride. *She forgot to invite the bride.*

Sofia added heavy cream to her shopping list, starring it and pumpkin as priorities. She looked forward to visiting the pumpkin patch just outside Cabot Falls. There was something satisfying about wandering up and down the colorful rows with a red Radio Flyer wagon to pick out her favorite gourds. It was the Halloween version of the Christmas tree farm.

She had just picked up the diary again when Marla rang her cell phone.

"I found an interesting article on the Web today," Marla said. "It's a new theory about why Henry VIII fathered only the one child that lived to maturity from each of the mothers. It's only a theory, of course, but the article mentions a blood disorder. They think he was Kell-positive. Of course, without his DNA, it's going to remain an unproven theory. But I think you should read it." Marla said she would email her the link to the story.

"Thanks. I'll try to read it before the kids get home and take over the computer."

She mixed a tuna fish spread, made herself a sandwich, and put the rest in the fridge for the kids' after-school snack. Then she carried her lunch and the diary to the basement family room to eat while she did research.

The article Marla sent suggested that the Kell antigen didn't affect the firstborn, which would explain why Catherine's daughter, Mary Tudor, survived but Catherine was unsuccessful in producing more children who lived. Anne Boleyn's daughter, Elizabeth, was the only successful birth for her. And Jane Seymour's only child, Edward, survived to precede Elizabeth to the throne for a brief period. None of those women had successful births after their first. Elizabeth Blount's son Henry Fitzroy was her only child with Henry, but she went on to have more children—not by King Henry—who matured and married.

This theory certainly made sense. Sofia could see why the scientists thought Henry must have been Kell-positive.

She bookmarked the website to reread after she had time to do more research. She wondered why Henry Fitzroy, as a first child, hadn't lived to maturity too. The diary mentioned poison. Had this been his fate? Or had the diabetes that historians said plagued the Tudor family killed him? There were so many things that might have claimed a young life back then, including the plague or even something they called the "sweating sickness," which was probably influenza or tuberculosis.

Yet *veleno* was written right there in the diary. It was Italian for "poison." And there was also *arsenico*, which unmistakably meant "arsenic."

The clock on the computer reminded Sofia that she had spent far too much time lost in speculation. Before she went upstairs, she retrieved the box of fall decorations from the storage closet. It was time to replace the cascade of purple asters with a russet-and-gold wreath, an assortment of gourds, and jack-o'-lanterns. She carried the box to the main floor just in time to hear the screech of wheels by someone in too much of a hurry. Fergus raced to the window, barking. Peering out the front window, she saw nothing.

Satisfied that it was safe, she disarmed the alarm and opened the door to replace the wreath. A paper fluttered to the stoop. The familiar scrawl sent a chill through her bones.

While she had been visiting the past, it seemed the dangers of the present had visited her. The note read, *I warned you.*

Windsor, England
Spring 1533

Maddalena was acutely aware that she was in danger as long as Rose blamed her for Thom Bell's incarceration. If angry looks were as lethal as the dagger the hotheaded young woman had strapped to her leg, then Maddalena's life was in jeopardy.

The fabric vault would be a perfect place for Rose to kill her. "Everyone knows that we are in here together," Maddalena reminded Rose. "And everyone heard you threaten me."

"I ain't the fool, Margaret. But I am patient." Rose gave Maddalena a hard shove against a row of fabric bolts leaning against the wall. One fell, and then another and another. Rose's hands were at Maddalena's throat. "But he ain't hanged yet, and I got me an idea how to save him. You better hope it works. If not . . ." She let her words fade as she loosened her grip. Maddalena understood.

It was useless to remind Rose that Thom was no good and didn't really love her. The two carried the heavy bolt of dark red velvet to the sewing room and lifted it to the cutting table. Rose drew her finger across her throat and smiled. "Until then, Margaret."

"Quit your chatter and lend an ear," Mabel said. "We must prepare a travel wardrobe for the king's visit to France. This will include multiple ensembles for His Grace, his son, and his lady."

"The queen?" Maddalena asked. No one had seen her in public since Christmas. Rumors indicated that she was gone and wouldn't return. Had Lucy's prediction been correct? Where was Queen Catherine?

"No," Mabel said. "I mean Lady Anne Boleyn. It is not our place to question or speculate, Margaret. Go to Lady Anne's chambers and return with measurements."

Maddalena listened intently, taking notes in her book as Lady Anne instructed her to make only the French-style caps and not the cathedral hoods worn by the English. Already she was distancing herself from the queen she had once served and now betrayed, the queen she fully intended to replace.

Maddalena tried to think of every reason to be positive about Queen Catherine. She reasoned that Lady Anne had spent most of her life in France, so perhaps the king was taking her along for her fluency in the language. But when Maddalena measured Lady Anne, her swollen waistline dispelled that theory. Lady Anne was with child.

What would this mean for Queen Catherine and her daughter? What would it mean for the ginger-haired boy who might one day be king?

Walking back to the sewing room, Maddalena felt heavy of heart. The queen had once told her that they had much in common. They were forced to live in a country other than that of their birth, and they were given names not their own. She thought of a third thing that they had in common: Their lives were in the hands of others.

And yet, neither had her future mapped out. Queen Catherine, according to palace gossip, refused to accept an annulment and had asked the Pope to intercede. King Henry wanted a solution to the matter by the time he returned.

As the days passed, castle whispers said that King Henry had secretly married Anne in the chapel to make sure the baby she carried would be a legitimate heir. Maddalena wondered how that could be when he was neither annulled nor divorced from Catherine.

Queen Catherine began to appear publicly at the cathedral and in the streets, where she was cheered and applauded by the people. This was an open rebuke of King Henry's demand for an annulment. Lady Anne, however, was jeered and insulted by the crowds. Had word of the secret marriage leaked from the confines of the castle?

By the time all the preparations for the king's journey were complete, summer was well underway. The king's dilemma was obvious even to Alice, who seemed to move through life wearing a blindfold. Certain of the outcome, Lady Anne instructed Maddalena to sketch ideas for what she might wear at her coronation upon their return to England.

When Maddalena brought Lady Anne her sketches, she found her gazing out the window with the curiosity of a cat watching a mouse, her hand resting protectively over her belly. When Maddalena approached, she caught a glimpse of the ginger-haired duke with the ready smile in the courtyard below. Lady Anne was no doubt imagining her place at the king's side, secure as the queen and then the queen mother. In her mind, the king had already cast the young Duke of Richmond aside along with Queen Catherine and his daughter Mary.

No wonder Maddalena's father could so easily leave his own daughter in the hands of strangers. As is the ruler, so are the subjects. At least the king could pretend that he had good reason—saving England for a male heir. But what of Maddalena's father? He had no such excuses. Yet she couldn't hate him. She could only pity him. *I will show you, Papa. I will not only survive, I will thrive—without you and without Allessandro, if I must.*

Lady Anne's pregnancy and the king's trip to France had the whole castle abuzz for weeks. Maddalena could scarcely turn a corner without someone catching her ear with another shocking story. Maddalena was looking forward to some calm after their departure. But then Mabel told her, "You and Rose will be in the king's entourage." Mabel was all business when she said it, but Maddalena thought she saw a hint of sympathy in her eyes. "Lady Anne expects you to make note of the fashions in the French court and be prepared to make alterations if necessary." Mabel sniffed as if she had detected something foul.

"Rose?" Maddalena questioned. "But . . ."

"You two are the fastest seamstresses. Alice is too slow, as now I am, and Lucy's mean streak is liable to burst forth at inopportune moments. Rose is the only other possibility."

As much as Maddalena didn't relish the thought of being alone with Rose, the idea that she would be on her own continent gave Maddalena hope. That a thousand miles or more lay between her and her beloved Venice and Allessandro was daunting, but not impossible. That night, while Alice got them their stew from the inn, she quickly counted out the meager coins she'd received for her service as a seamstress. After Alice fell asleep, she would sew them into the hem of her smock. Would it be enough to pay her way on a caravan returning to Venice?

Alice was fretful that she would be left alone. She seemed to grow stranger each day, and more and more, Maddalena came to understand why the others called her daft. "The trip is only a month," she reassured the older woman. "We will return before you miss my company." *That is, if I cannot find a way home,* she thought guiltily.

Maddalena stood near the back of the ship, watching as the white cliffs grew distant and less distinguished. How excited she had been the first time she saw them a lifetime ago!

"Homesick already?"

Startled from her thoughts, Maddalena curtsied just as a whitecap rocked the ship, and she tumbled to the deck.

"Oh, Mad Margaret, let me help you to your feet," the young duke said. "You were never meant for all of this royal nonsense, were you?"

She focused her eyes on the scarred toes of his boots. "Your Grace, I apologize. I didn't realize who you were until the games. I never meant any disrespect."

He took her chin, much as Allessandro used to, so that she was directly facing him. "I am truly sorry that you found out. I rather liked your show of independence. I envy that." His lips curled in a smile, but his eyes showed a depth of sadness, of pain, that she had not noticed before.

"Envy me, Your Grace?" Maddalena felt a sudden and overwhelming pity for him. He was in a purgatory of his own, caught between a royal and an outcast, teetering on the brink, as unsure of his fate as his stepmother, Queen Catherine, was of him. They were the same, and yet they were adversaries. Queen Catherine wanted to remain queen to save the throne for her daughter, Mary. Yet this boy, through no fault of his own, was caught between two strong women who wished he didn't exist. His position was even more precarious than Maddalena's.

"God be with you, Your Grace," Maddalena blurted out. She gasped, shocked that her thoughts had found voice.

"And with you, Mad Margaret." He gave her a long look. "Maddalena Vitari."

She watched as Henry, Duke of Richmond and Somerset, walked away, leaving her to her own thoughts. He had a grace and dignity beneath his youthful cheeriness. No wonder he was popular among his people, despite his unorthodox claim to the throne. Had he been a daughter, he would have been cast aside without a thought. Yet, as the only surviving male, he was King Henry's pride. *Unless the baby Anne carries is a son. How fickle fate is. How uncertain our destinies.*

She shook her head in dismay. Could it really be that both of them had no control over their fates? Maddalena found this hard to accept.

She had no sooner shoved those thoughts from her mind than Rose appeared on deck.

"It would be so easy to send you over the side," Rose said, her voice carrying on the breeze. "But 'twould only double me work."

"Rose, for the last time, I am not the cause of Thom's troubles. They didn't even care that he tried to attack me. They were concerned only for the king's silver spoons. He is a thief and a bully."

A low rumble in Rose's throat grew into an alarming growl, and Maddalena braced herself as Rose rushed at her. At the last moment, she stepped aside. Rose slammed into the railing with such force that her feet left the deck. She rolled forward, shrieking. Maddalena grabbed her, holding with all her might and pulling Rose back over the railing.

Rose sat on the deck of the ship and caught her breath. When she could manage it, she looked up at Maddalena and spoke. "Why did you stop me?"

Maddalena was surprised by the question. "Why would I not stop you? We are both caught up in circumstances. But we have choices. We don't have to be adversaries. We are the same."

"We ain't the same, Miss 'igh-and-Mighty. All I 'ave is Thom, and now I don't 'ave 'im at all! You may think I owe you a favor now, but I don't. We ain't through." She got to her feet and stalked away.

The ship was suddenly abuzz with activity as the seamen shouted, racing about to moor. Sighing heavily, Maddalena hurried forward. Before her lay the city of Calais. She could only hope that it would bring solutions, not more problems.

9

Cabot Falls, Vermont
Present Day

Sofia stood on the stoop as the stench of burning tires lingered in the air. She stared down at the note: *You were warned.*

As the yapping of the Coopers' miniature poodle got louder, she looked up. Pat Cooper was speed-walking in her direction, their little dog, Willow, at her heels, sounding like a lawnmower in distress.

Inside, Fergus barked his warning as if to say, "My house."

Pat arrived breathlessly. "I heard tires squealing. Did you see what happened?"

Numbly, Sofia shook her head no. "I think they left this." She held the note at one corner near the edge as if it were a ticking time bomb. In a way it was.

"Then I won't touch it. Call Ryan. The driver left trace evidence this time." She pointed triumphantly toward the street. Pat was using her growing crime vocabulary for the black streak on the street.

Sofia could feel her blood pulsing through her temples. "Come on in, Pat, while I try to get ahold of him."

"Home," Pat told the dog. "Home."

Whimpering a protest, Willow tucked tail and trotted off toward the Cooper residence. It seemed even the feisty dog was intimidated by the retired English teacher.

Inside, Sofia dialed the direct number Officer Quimby had given her in case of trouble. This certainly qualified. "I've received another warning note, and this time it was left on my door," she told the officer.

Pat signaled that she wanted to talk, and Sofia handed the phone to her.

"Ryan, it's Mrs. Cooper. Don't park directly in front of the house. And bring some orange cones. We don't want anyone overlaying the tire tracks, now do we? When can you get here?"

Sofia had to hand it to Pat; she got what she demanded of people. Before the chamomile tea was ready, the doorbell rang. Officer Quimby had already blocked off the rubber streak with cones. He peered over Sofia's shoulder to where his former English teacher sat, and his shoulders sagged visibly. It was obvious to Sofia that it was hard being a grown-up officer and not a little boy playing cop in Pat's presence.

The teapot whistled and Sofia motioned for Quimby to follow. She laid out three mugs and a plate full of banana-nut muffins. The officer used a latex glove to put the note in an evidence bag. "Chances are we won't get a good print or it won't be in the system," he said. "Without a comparison, we can't identify the subject."

"What about the tire tracks, dear?" Pat Cooper wanted to know.

"It's not like on television. We're just a little village where the worst crime of the day is usually a damaged mailbox or a dog digging up the neighbor's flowers."

"We understand," Sofia said in an attempt to restore his dignity.

"I have a book with hundreds of tire tread samples. It'll take time for me to look through and compare."

"Oh, pishposh, Ryan. What about the FBI? It would take them only a few minutes."

"Yes, ma'am. B-but it's not exactly high priority." Officer

Quimby was starting to stutter again under Pat's pressure.

"It's high priority with the Parker family," Sofia said. Then she added, "Tea's ready!"

"I'd better get this stuff in to the lab," he said as he pushed back his chair.

"Oh, sit, dear," Pat said. "Every cop gets a code seven now and then." She turned to Sofia. "That's a meal break."

Officer Quimby surrendered to his old teacher and slid back into his chair, muttering about chain of evidence. After a few minutes, Pat excused him. They watched from the window as he measured and photographed the track, then left.

"He's a good cop," Pat said on her way out the door.

Sofia made sandwiches for the kids and stowed them in the fridge. She grabbed her coat and keys and double-checked the door lock before pulling out of her drive. She trusted that Pat would keep an eye out for the culprit who had inserted himself into their lives. Having a retired busybody neighbor did have its advantages.

She joined the line of cars waiting in front of the three-story brick school as Vanessa peeled off from a group of giggling girls and walked past a trio of boys who stared after her. As a mother, it was hard to get used to that.

Wynter was already at the sidewalk and hopped inside first. "I know what you're going to say, Mom. But I saw you coming."

Vanessa stopped to speak to her boyfriend, and Sofia honked, setting off a cacophony of horns that weren't to be outdone. Her daughter got in the vehicle beside Wynter in the backseat. "This is so embarrassing. I don't know why I can't ride with Ethan."

Without answering, Sofia put the Suburban into gear and headed to the nearby middle school. Two kids down and two to go. Maybe after she told them of the newest note, they wouldn't resent her ruining their social images so much. Sofia felt like Fergus, herding a bunch of obstinate goats. She hoped that the "trace evidence" would provide answers.

When someone had the nerve to come right up to the door and leave a note, it was just too close for comfort.

Calais, France
Spring 1533

Maddalena felt uncomfortable in the extreme, being so close to the monarch's inner circle. King Henry's erratic behavior made her feel unsafe. A man who would exile his wife and ban her from public view while he took Lady Anne Boleyn with him, bold as you please, to Calais was not to be trusted. And yet, here they were, in a city the English called "the brightest jewel in the English crown" despite its location across the channel and attached to France.

"It is a complicated game of chess played by the monarchs," one of King Francis's servants told her as he directed Maddalena and Rose to their quarters. "Each one lays a claim to Pas-de-Calais. The truth is, the ferrymen are the real winners. Both monarchs pay dearly for the passage for themselves and their many servants." He chuckled. "But for practical purposes, you are still subject to your English king's rules."

Maddalena smiled. She understood that while the common people lived in the reality of poverty and anxiety, the monarchs lived in denial and delusion. How else could King Henry believe himself to be infallible and simply commandeer the Church and its clergy so that he could fool himself into believing his marriage to Queen Catherine was invalid? How else could he so callously isolate her from everyone she loved, simply because she would not forsake her vows? And all for that woman the balladeers made fun of and the commoners called a sorceress—and worse! "Water is water," Maddalena replied. "It knows not what it is called or who believes they own it. It merely obeys nature and the moon."

The quarters were better than she had with Alice, although she was wary of sleep with Rose in the room. King Francis was not the grandiose host his English counterpart was, but the meals and entertainment were elegant to behold. From her vantage point hidden in the shadows of a heavily draped doorway, Maddalena observed Lady Anne Boleyn obviously basking in her prematurely assumed role of queen.

Never mind that the king was a bigamist in the eyes of the Church and his people. He wanted the child—a son, he hoped—to be legitimate.

As an artist, Maddalena observed how people unwittingly seemed to send out secret messages that conflicted with their verbal messages. Maddalena noted that the young Duke of Richmond, the king's natural son, smiled and participated at the left hand of his father, all while leaning away, creating a symbolic gap between them—together, yet apart.

To Maddalena, King Henry and her father merged into one person. It was getting harder to remember what Orsino Vitari looked like. Was it the distance and time that had caused him to fade? No. She could still clearly see Allessandro in her mind's eye, imagine his lips on her cheek, and hear his voice speaking of love and the future. Perhaps it was the fact that her father was becoming less important to her future than she had ever thought possible.

The Venetian ambassador, Sebastian Giustiniani, joined the celebrations on the third night. Despite her best efforts, Maddalena could find no reasonable excuse to be near him. Finally, during a break in the events, Maddalena approached his apartment and begged his secretary to give her an audience with the ambassador.

The secretary refused her request, as she suspected he would. She pleaded with him to allow her to see the man but was dismissed with a wave. She tried to explain her situation to the secretary, but he cut her off curtly: "Go now, or I will have you taken away."

Frustrated, desperate, and exhausted from lack of sleep, Maddalena took a chance. "As a citizen of the Republic of Venice," she said as loudly as she could, "I demand that you take my request to the most honorable ambassador."

"Antonio!" The shout came from inside the visitor's apartment. "What is going on out there?"

The secretary disappeared into the apartment, closing the door so that Maddalena could not hear. She had almost convinced herself that she had nothing to lose by bursting through the door uninvited when it swung open and the secretary, looking chagrined, motioned for her to enter.

Ambassador Giustiniani peered at documents and, without looking up, dismissed the secretary with a wave of his hand. He sat at a handsomely carved desk that reminded her of the one her father brought back from one of his trips to the Orient. She stood waiting for the man to look up, growing more impatient and annoyed at his inaction. Venetians were mannered and courtly, if anything. This man was making it clear that she was of no consequence to him. She shifted her weight from one foot to the other until she could no longer tolerate the silence. "Signore Ambassador."

When he failed to react she spoke more clearly. "Signore Ambassador, as a citizen of the Republic of Venice, I—"

"You what?" He leaned back in his chair, crossing his arms over his chest. His expression as he scanned her was one of contempt.

Maddalena could feel her face flush. "I expect the respect I am owed as a Venetian. I expect the simple courtesy for which our gentlemen are noted. I expect you to ignore the humble clothes I wear through no choice of my own. And I expect you to listen to what I have to say."

The ambassador's jaw sagged as he stood and motioned to the sitting area. He waited until she had taken a tufted parlor chair before seating himself opposite her. "And you are . . . ?"

"I am Maddalena Vitari, daughter of Orsino Vitari, merchant." She thought she detected a glint of recognition in his eyes. She was counting on her father's reputation as a friend of the doge to gain a foothold in the conversation, and it seemed to work. She continued, "I seek passage with your entourage to return to Venice under your protection."

"If you are truly who you say you are, how did you come to"—he gestured at her peasant clothes—"this?"

"It is a longer story than you obviously have time for. Suffice it to say, I was separated from my father's entourage when it departed, and I seek your help to return home."

"This is most unorthodox," he replied. She could see ambivalence in his expression.

"I will pay you a small advance. Whatever else is owed will be paid when I reach home." She was sure that no matter how her father felt about her uninvited return, he would pay the ambassador in order to stay on the good side of government. She had no doubt that the ambassador, no matter what his position, would not turn away any amenities.

Her seamstress earnings were small, but they would do as a token of good faith, an advance against the full amount. She smiled reassuringly at him.

The ambassador nodded. "We leave at first light. I will inform the secretary to expect you and your stipend."

Maddalena thanked him and left. Her feet felt lighter than they had at any time since she first arrived. She was going home! She could deal with her father when she got there.

Maddalena hurried through the narrow streets back to the quarters she shared with Rose. She untied the wool cloth she used to hold her changes of clothes and pulled out her smock. "No no no *no!*"

The hem was ripped open. The coins she'd sewn into it were gone. All of them—gone. "No!" Without the advance, her hopes of returning with the ambassador's entourage were dashed.

Maddalena knew it was of no use, but she spread the fabric on the mattress and shook each garment to be sure. The money was not there. Who would do such a thing?

Rose! It must have been Rose. So that was the plan she spoke of.

She turned to Rose's bed, but her knapsack of clothes was gone. She must have taken the money and hurried back to Windsor to beat the hangman's noose. She was going to bribe a prison guard to leave Thom's cage open and look the other way.

Blinded by her own tears, Maddalena stumbled out of the room and down the corridor. She had to get her money back, and she had to get it before morning, when the ambassador's group would leave.

Maddalena frantically raced through the corridors of the servants' area, looking for Rose. *The ferry!* It was the only way back.

Maddalena scampered through the streets of the town, dodging pedestrians and carts and ignoring the angry shouts of those she passed. She could see at the end of the street a ferry at the dock. People milled on its deck. Its gate was closed. Her breath came in short, painful bursts and her heart thumped against her rib cage. Her ankles throbbed as she pounded across the cobblestones.

She was no more than fifty yards away when she saw the ferry pull away from the dock. She was too late. She could see Rose standing at the aft rail, arms crossed defiantly. Maddalena collapsed in a breathless heap. She wept uncontrollably. "Rose, how could you? How could you be so cruel?" At this moment she hated Rose, even as she understood why the girl had done it. She would risk many things to save Allessandro—perhaps even steal to save him from the hangman's noose.

Still, she couldn't help but worry about the foolish girl. Rose would be a fugitive, wanted for the rest of her life, and all because of a man who was not worth the trouble. Would her pittance mean the difference between Thom hanging and going free? Rose had to be at her wits' end to risk everything, including prison. And justice had no qualms about hanging a woman either.

Taking a deep breath, Maddalena stood and brushed the dust from her skirt. She realized that she must consider her own dilemma now. The ambassador had made it clear that she had to pay her way, and now she had nothing to offer. There was nothing to do but continue in the service of King Henry and begin once more. She could not take the ferry to catch Rose. Even if she could pay the fee, she'd never be able to catch up with her before she spent the money. Maddalena would have to wait until the household returned to Windsor. By then, Rose would be gone, probably disappeared into the countryside with Thom.

Maddalena realized that her bold plan had failed.

10

Cabot Falls, Vermont
Present Day

Sofia hadn't heard anything from Officer Quimby after two days. She tried to concentrate on counting out the Halloween napkins and table linens to assure her there were enough for Gretchen's luncheon. Vanessa had done a really good job on them. The aunts would be so proud of her.

Wynter had folded them and tucked the flatware inside, which would make it easy for Sofia on the day of the event. Vanessa had suggested that Sofia serve the pumpkin soup from a real pumpkin, so Jim figured out the dimensions she'd need to fit the slow cooker inside it. Her family had been great helps in getting the October activities under control.

Sofia settled on *rosa di Parma* tenderloin since it was a simple but showy dish suitable for a luncheon. It was a tradition for celebrations in the Parma province in Italy. *Scapece* pumpkin with pasta, a green salad, and soft breadsticks would be perfect with it. For dessert, there would be the ridiculous pumpkin-head bride-and-groom cake. Sofa was making a list of the ingredients to buy when the doorbell rang.

Julie and Marla stood on the stoop, paint supplies and wine in hand. Sofia blinked to wipe away what must surely be an apparition. "Paint day?" she asked meekly. She had totally disregarded the calendar and the big red circle around the date.

"Are you okay?" Marla asked. "It's not like you to forget, Sofia. If it's a bad day—"

"No, no, come on in and set up. Here, let me open the wine to breathe." Sofia left the painters to set up and went into the kitchen.

Unwrapping a lemon loaf she retrieved from the freezer, she set it in the microwave with a custard cup of water and set it for defrost. When the carousel rumbled to life, she turned around, sucking in her breath. "Oh! I didn't hear you come in."

"Something is definitely wrong," Marla said, standing a few feet away. "Spill it, girl. We know how to listen, and we know how to keep secrets. What's that saying about a shared burden being only half as heavy?"

"Right. Let's paint, and I'll talk." Sofia followed Marla into the four-season room. Julie had already kicked off her patent leather heels and stood barefoot, a smock over her houndstooth sheath.

"All right, girlfriend, no more stalling," Julie said. "It's time to share."

"What's bothering you?" Marla added.

Sofia told them about the notes and the dark SUV. "It is all so bizarre. I mean, we live G-rated lives."

"Are you sure you aren't just building mountains out of anthills?" Julie asked.

"Molehills," Marla said.

"It's too unbelievable that a nice, average, boring family like yours could attract somebody that mean."

"Boring? Thanks a lot, Julie!" Sofia chided. "And you're in public relations?" She laughed. "It does seem ridiculous on the surface. My ancestors must think we've turned into a bunch of dullards, considering how exciting their lives were." She couldn't imagine her family in the presence of kings and killers. Having a stalker that hid behind cryptic notes was bad enough.

"That reminds me," Marla said. She dug into her purse and

pulled out a rolled paper with a rubber band around it. "I found this in one of the art books and made a copy for you. Maybe it will ease your mind about the green square on the quilt."

Sofia slid the rubber band off and unrolled the paper. It showed a group of men with bows and arrows atop jet-black horses. They wore green clothes that looked to be from the sixteenth century. "It doesn't appear to be signed or dated, and it's kind of blurry. For all I can tell, it could be a paint-by-numbers project," she said.

"That was as clear as I could get it. The library scanner isn't great at copying photos. The painting was actually hanging on the wall behind the photo of a collector of antique correspondence. There was a sudden rush at the counter, and when I had time to look again, someone had checked it out. I remember the publisher, though. I'll see if they can put me in contact with the collector. At least it appears to validate the color mentioned in the diary." Marla sounded disappointed that Sofia wasn't more excited.

"You're right, of course," Sofia said. "It's a clue worthy of follow-up." *Speaking of clues, why hasn't Officer Quimby called?* It was hard to concentrate on anything else. That stalker had done more than leave notes and skulk around. He had stolen her peace of mind.

Windsor, England
Spring 1533

The order to prepare for departure from Calais spread

through the servants' quarters. The coronation of Anne Boleyn was set for the last day of May. There were clothes to create for those attending and a special dress for Anne. Before they left for France, the king had commanded Mabel to oversee the creation of a black nightgown, a wedding gift for the bride. He wanted it ready upon his return from the state visit with King Francis.

He had proclaimed himself the head of the Church of England and no longer under the power of the papacy. The priests and monks continued as they always had, so it was difficult for the subjects to see any difference. The real change was that King Henry could push through an annulment from his marriage to Queen Catherine, even without her consent or acceptance. He would be free to announce his secret January marriage to Lady Anne with an unburdened conscience.

Maddalena wondered what she should tell anyone when they missed Rose. She needn't have worried. The gossipmongers were so busy whispering about the king and his consort that they talked of little else.

During the crossing, Maddalena sat on the deck, sketching the faces of the sailors. Their rugged looks and their expressions as they worked intrigued her.

She noticed the Duke of Richmond leaning on the rail, gazing out over the water. He was particularly handsome in his pensive mood, and she sketched his likeness into her book. She was filling in shading detail when a shadow fell across her page.

It was the duke. Maddalena scrambled to her feet and curtsied. "Oh, forgive me, Your Grace. If you wish for me to destroy—"

"That is very good, Maddalena. See? A true artist should be called by her true name."

She smiled. "Thank you." She tore it from her book and offered it to him. "It's yours."

"That is kind of you. I will give it to my mother. Would I

insult you if I offered a small token of appreciation? I believe that artists should receive recompense for their efforts."

"A token?"

"Just a shilling, although your work is worth much more. May I see your book?"

"It would be my honor." Maddalena had not thought about selling her sketches. They seemed so—so unfinished. She had fallen into the habit of sketching faces and scenes so that she might paint them later, and she considered them only tools of her work. She held her breath, remembering the true but perhaps less-flattering sketches of his father and of Lady Anne.

"You capture so much more than features, Maddalena. It is as if you peered into their thoughts. We all have many faces—the face we show people of great authority, the face we show our peers, and the face we have when we think we are alone."

She wondered which face she had sketched of the duke. She saw pain on his face, a free soul wounded by circumstances. Once they reached Windsor, Lady Anne would be crowned. Henry had ordered Queen Catherine to call herself Dowager Princess of Wales and enter a convent. By refusing to annul their marriage, she'd lost everything but her pride. Maddalena realized that surely the duke understood what was in store for him once the legitimate royal infant arrived—especially if it was the much-coveted male child.

Perhaps he would be better for it. As he was pushed farther from the throne, the pressure assuredly would be lessened. Wrenched from his mother's arms at birth to live what many wrongly believed was the ideal and prestigious life, he appeared pressured beyond all others.

Maddalena would not trade lives with him, even though hers was also oppressed and lonely.

When she returned to the palace, Mabel called her aside.

"Where is Rose? She was with you on the journey, was she not?"

Maddalena flushed. No matter what she thought of Rose, she didn't want to tell Mabel what had happened. "Yes, she went to Calais with us. I have not seen her since returning." There. She had not lied, and she had not told.

Mabel rested a bony hand on Maddalena's arm. "I fear that she is in for a donkey's load of trouble. I heard rumors that Thom Bell escaped from the prison, and I am afraid that Rose is with him." Her hand dropped to her side. "The little fool. Well, we'll simply have to bring in a new apprentice, or work harder. That woman is demanding a new wardrobe for her coronation, and there is little time to complete it."

Maddalena felt dumbfounded. Had Mabel just called the queen-to-be *that woman*?

"When you say your prayers, keep Rose in mind," Mabel said. "If God watches over the sparrow, then there is hope for Rose."

It was the first kind quality Maddalena had witnessed in the time-hardened Mabel. But she was right. Rose could expect only disappointment and heartache from Thom. She had been better off when he was in prison—or better yet, at the end of the hangman's noose. Bitterness crept into her thoughts. Yet Rose was also a thief. Perhaps they deserved each other.

Lady Anne's changing body was an ill-kept secret. By the coronation, even the least observant would know. Maddalena stood waiting for Mabel to dismiss her, but Mabel seemed lost in her own thoughts as she stared out the window. Maddalena followed her gaze and saw that a small gray bird pecked at the pane, strutting back and forth on the ledge.

"There is one more thing," Mabel said at last. "Can I trust you, Margaret?" She looked fretful.

Maddalena could see that whatever was on Mabel's mind, it was serious. She felt a rush of compassion for the older woman.

"I give you my word that I will not betray you, whatever you say."

"There is a mission of mercy. I will not command you to make it. You may refuse, and I will think nothing less of you."

"What is it?" Maddalena asked. "I can see that it is important to you. Whatever it is, I will do it. I promise."

Mabel looked about and then spoke. "The king has sent Queen Catherine to Manor of the More, a horrible place to live. She will need warmer garments and fur throws. Everyone is forbidden to visit her or to aid her in any way. As a foreigner, you have a better chance to go without punishment if you were caught. I would go myself, but . . ."

"I understand," Maddalena said. "Will you make the travel arrangements? I don't know who I can trust."

"On the first of May, it is traditional for ladies of the court to go into the countryside and gather the morning dew to use for their complexions all year. Meanwhile, we will have to work quickly to prepare the coronation wardrobes, especially since we will not have Rose's help. There will be too much activity; we will wait until the festivities leading up to the coronation. All attention will be focused on the court. I will tell Alice that I am sending you to gather woad so that we may dye some fabrics. On the day of the coronation, a carriage will wait for you at the Lane's End. It will be difficult to make the trip in a day's turnaround, but if it is any longer, others will ask questions we will not want to answer. Is that clear?"

For most of the country the coronation was blasphemy, and the people went about their business as usual on that day. Only in the palace and in the cathedral, where the bells rang out the news, did the castle intrigue seem to matter. That was, except to Maddalena, who bade goodbye to Alice at early light and hurried to the edge of town where a carriage already filled with the furs and other aids for Queen Catherine waited. Nervous at first, and sure that every eye was on her, Maddalena soon relaxed and enjoyed the journey.

The air changed drastically as the scenery went from shady forests teeming with birds to ominous stands of leafless skeleton trees. A musky smell permeated the air, eventually emitting a sour smell of decay. Maddalena felt rawness in her throat, and it was difficult to swallow.

Manor of the More was surrounded by soggy peat bogs and foul swamp. There was neither a bird's song nor a scampering squirrel. There was no life at all except for the croak of a frog before some horrid, slithering thing silenced it with one snap of its jaws. The air was dank, and the moisture crept through Maddalena's clothes. It seeped into her bones, and she shivered fiercely before relenting and wrapping herself in the furs meant for the queen.

The castle was plain, and the view from the windows would surely be depressing. There was no garden in which to stroll, no seats on which to sit. It was desolate and foreboding, but no more so than the man who would send the woman he shared a kingdom with for nearly a quarter of a century here.

Maddalena felt overwhelming compassion for the strong woman who would endure this rather than forsake her marriage vows and title and her daughter's rightful heritage. The carriage halted in front of the steps, and a woman answered the door, a startled look on her face.

"Please help me bring in supplies. I've brought a few things for Her Grace." Maddalena handed a fox-fur coverlet to the woman, who buried her face in it momentarily. The woman smiled. "It is so good to see an unfamiliar face. And how wonderful that the king has shown mercy on—"

"I'm afraid that I come in secret and with some risk," Maddalena interrupted. "The seamstress Mabel thought the queen might need a few things." She glanced around. The place was as barren and bleak inside as it was out.

"I'm Cadence. It has been so long since we have had news from the outside," the woman said.

"I am afraid that any news I bring would not be welcomed," Maddalena replied. "If the queen wishes, however, I am willing to speak with her."

"Wait here. I will see." Cadence disappeared up the stairs and returned quickly. "Yes, please come with me."

Maddalena followed Cadence to a room on the upper floor. Seated in a parlor chair near the window was Queen Catherine, stitching on a tapestry. She was pale and thin, but she still looked as regal and in charge as she did in the portraits King Henry had removed to the storage rooms to be replaced by those of his new queen. Gone were the many attendants who had giggled and swarmed about her. If there were servants other than Cadence, they were not visible.

"Come, child. Sit here with me. Cadence will bring us tea. Tell me news. We hear so little." She waited until Cadence had poured the tea and left the room before speaking again. "Tell me about my husband. Is he well? I have not seen him since Christmas."

"Yes, Your Highness. I am not privy to his health and do not see him." Maddalena studied the queen's face. Was this a game of pretend, or had she gone daft, living so isolated in this swamp? *Is denial how she survives?*

"I have not had any response to my letters. I must assume

that he is quite busy with affairs of state." The queen's body was still straight and proud, but the depth of darkness in her eyes seemed to say that she knew it was a farce, a play of the absurd. "My daughter, Mary—have you heard any news of her?"

The tea was weak and unsweetened, almost tasteless. Maddalena assumed that the leaves were used many times in brewing. She felt the urge to lay her hand on the thin, pale hand of the queen, to offer her comfort, yet she dared not. "I understand that she travels, Your Highness." At the command of the king, of course. She, too, had been exiled and was not even allowed to see her mother. King Henry knew no limits to his cruelty in punishing this woman.

"By your leave, Your Highness, I must be traveling. We will be on the road a long while," Maddalena said. She realized that she was the only visitor who had seen the queen in so long. She felt sad that she had to leave her, but she dared stay no longer, else some of the sad news from the court would slip out.

She was glad to leave the demoralizing landscape. It smelled of death. How could the fragile woman continue on for very long in those circumstances of isolation and deprivation? Maddalena resolved to no longer feel sorry for her own circumstances.

The carriage sway lulled her into an uneasy sleep until she was jolted awake, nearly tumbling from the seat. The carriage door swung open. "There is an incident on the road," her driver said. "Perhaps you'd like to walk about while I see to the delay."

He offered her a hand, and Maddalena stepped onto the rutted road. It was dark. Maddalena hadn't realized that she'd slept so long. Just ahead, a group of men stood around something in the road. They held lanterns and mumbled among themselves.

"What is happening?" Maddalena asked.

One of the men turned to her. "Daniel found a woman at the side of the road. Dead. A shame. She was a pretty little thing."

Maddalena came closer and then gasped. This was no stranger. "Rose!" Maddalena's breath caught in her throat. "It was Thom that killed her. It had to be." She wondered how the others would take the news.

11

Cabot Falls, Vermont
Present Day

$\mathcal{S}$ofia grabbed the phone the moment it rang, hoping for news from Officer Quimby. She tried to hide her disappointment that it was Marla.

"The book arrived this morning," Marla said. "You said your ancestor's name was Vitari? I checked the port records during Henry's reign, and I found an Orsino Vitari, merchant, listed in 1532 with cargo charges for bolts of fabric. He was listed every year for over a decade. I didn't find any after 1537, so either he retired or died. Sometimes ships sank in storms. The logs list him as a citizen of Venice."

"Then that has to be my ancestor. A fabric merchant would make sense. I think you're onto something. Did it mention a daughter or wife?"

"No, but he was also charged for five more passengers. But maybe one of them is a daughter. There's no way to tell from this."

"Darn. I was hoping for something more definitive," Sofia said.

"Sometimes you have to be a good detective. Follow clues and piece them together with logic and common sense."

"I'll pick up the book before noon," Sofia promised. "And thanks again. I appreciate the help."

Sofia paired her gray slacks with her blue plaid shirt and topped it with the solid blue corduroy shirt. There was a damp chill in the

111

air from the dew on the ground. She slipped into her all-weather Mary Janes as she considered the sailing manifest. She wondered how one of her ancestors could leave his own daughter on one of those trips. It was so heartless, even in an era when women were considered property instead of individuals with rights.

The cold bit her cheeks as she shut the front door behind her and quick-stepped down the sidewalk to the Chevy Suburban. As Sofia backed out, she spotted a dark SUV across the street in the cul-de-sac.

"I'm sick of this," she muttered. She put the Suburban into park but left the motor running. Stepping out of the car, she touched two fingers near her eyes and then pointed them straight at the SUV, giving the signal that every child recognized as "I'm watching you."

The SUV bolted around the corner and headed toward town. "Not this time," Sofia said. "Let the hunted become the hunter." She jumped into her vehicle and headed in the same direction.

The SUV was nowhere in sight. She pulled over and dialed her neighbor and told her what had happened. "I'm running errands now. Can you keep an eye on things for a while?"

"Copy that," Pat replied eagerly.

Fretting that she had lost the SUV, but relieved that it hadn't come to more of a confrontation, Sofia continued to the library.

"Good news!" Marla exclaimed as Sofia approached the checkout desk. "The book is back. I bookmarked the page for you."

Sofia moved to one of the reading tables and sat down with the book spread open in front of her. The clothes were definitely sixteenth century. The hunting party was mixed gender, and they were all dressed in green. The central figure seemed more elegantly clothed than the others. But the photograph was focused on the collector. Everything else was fuzzy.

"Either the signature is obscured by the frame or the artist didn't sign and date it," she told Marla. "I'll try to contact the guy. If I can't authenticate the quilt square, I'll be so disappointed." It would spoil a perfectly good family legend.

Outside, Sofia checked her cell phone. What was taking Quimby so long? Surely it had been enough time.

She stopped at the post office for stamps and picked up a few things at the grocer's before heading home again. She repeatedly checked the rearview mirror to be sure she wasn't being followed. Maybe her little act of bravery earlier had scared the culprit away for good, although she doubted that it was that easy.

On the Road to Windsor, England
Spring 1533

Maddalena couldn't take her eyes off Rose's lifeless body. How could she not have predicted that her choices would have tragic consequences?

A man approached on horseback, and one of the onlookers said it was the sheriff. Maddalena introduced herself. "Her name is Rose Styles. She is—was—a seamstress at Windsor Castle. I believe that she was traveling with Thom Bell, a former butcher at the castle and an escapee from prison. I don't know if she met her fate at his hands, or if they were attacked by highwaymen. I do, however, suspect the former."

"And how do you know all this?" he asked.

Maddalena tried to present the kind of dignity and grace she had witnessed in Queen Catherine only hours ago. "I am a seamstress at Windsor Castle."

The sheriff narrowed his eyes, studying her curiously. "Then what are you doing out here on the road alone?"

"I am not alone. And the king's business is none of yours—except when one of his subjects is so callously murdered," she bluffed.

He doffed his hat, mockingly. "I am sorry to have offended you. You know this Thom Bell? How do you know that he was with her?"

"Because she'd planned to bribe Thom's way out of prison. She loved him, poor woman," Maddalena said. She did not tell him about Rose's theft. What purpose would it achieve?

"Since you know so much, can you tell me where I might find this Thom Bell? How will I recognize him?"

"I can do better than that," Maddalena said. "Let me fetch my sketchbook from the carriage."

When she returned, she requested that one of the men hold his lantern near. Thumbing through her book, she found the sketch of Thom. It captured the sneer of his mouth and the ominous glint in his eyes, like a cat about to pounce on its prey. She ripped it from her book and handed it to the sheriff. "I hope you find him, although I imagine he is far away from here by now. He is evil through and through."

By then, the men had wrapped Rose's body in bunting and placed it in a wagon.

"What will happen to her?" Maddalena asked.

"Is there family at Windsor?"

"As I recall, she is orphaned," Maddalena replied.

"Then it's a pauper's grave here, I suppose," the sheriff replied. "We'll look for Bell, but he may have headed to friends."

"I doubt he has any," Maddalena replied. She boarded the carriage, and the driver urged the horses forward.

There were no further incidents on the road, and Maddalena arrived well after Alice had retired for the night.

She woke the next morning and braced for the questions she would face.

"Where is the woad?" Alice asked. "You were gone far too long. I was concerned for your safety."

"I did not find any," Maddalena replied. She hated lying, and she couldn't look Alice in the eyes.

"What do you mean, you couldn't find any? It is everywhere this time of year. Do you even know what it looks like? I should have gone with you." Alice wrung her hands fretfully.

Maddalena wished that she could tell Alice the truth, but the woman was unstable. What if Alice were to say something to the wrong person?

"There was an incident," Maddalena said. "But I want to wait until we are with the others. I don't think I can bear to tell it more than once."

Lucy and Mabel were already in the sewing room when Maddalena and Alice arrived. An older woman with tendrils of gray hair protruding from her cap was introduced as Joan Baker. She seemed old for an apprentice, but Mabel explained that she was especially talented at working with silk and would help out until she found an apprentice—or until Rose returned.

"I am afraid I have bad news about Rose," Maddalena said. "She is dead. Murdered. I suspect that it was at the hands of Thom Bell."

She told them what she had witnessed.

"You know a good deal about it, don't you?" Lucy said. "I know how you felt about her. I heard you two arguing a lot. Maybe it was you who did her in." She threw back her head in a cackling laugh.

Maddalena shook her head. "That's vicious. How could you say that? Maybe I didn't like her, but—"

"Where were you yesterday?" Lucy demanded. "Did you follow her and Thom?"

"Lucy, think what you are saying," Maddalena demanded.

"Then where is the woad? Rose said you were jealous. She said you had designs on Thom."

"That is not true," Maddalena said, casting a glance at Mabel. Why didn't the woman speak up? "Thom was a terrible man, a thief and maybe a murderer. She should never have stolen my money to bail him out."

She stopped short. She'd just told everyone that Rose had stolen her money. It was a perfect motive for murder. Palace walls had ears and the corridors carried whispers like flotsam on the river. It was only a matter of time before the sheriff of Windsor would come for her. But what would she tell him? She was sworn to secrecy about her visit to Queen Catherine, and it was the only alibi she could offer.

It was past noon when the sound of boots on the marble floors echoed through the corridor outside the sewing room. Maddalena braced herself for what was to come.

The man's brown leather tunic and the sword at his side gave evidence that her worst fear had come to pass. "Maddalena Vitari, come into the corridor," he said.

Mabel stood, protesting. "Sheriff, no." Her eyes darted, and she blinked rapidly.

Maddalena touched her arm. "It is all right. I am safe. The truth is on my side." At least she hoped so. It had not done her much good of late. She followed the man into the corridor. "Sheriff, whatever you have heard, I assure you that it is Thom Bell you should be after."

"He is a bad sort and an escapee, I will not deny that. But there are witnesses that say you and Rose were seen arguing here and in Calais. And now you accuse her of theft. No one saw you at Windsor yesterday. Where were you?"

Maddalena closed her eyes and shook her head before replying.

"I cannot tell you." She had promised Mabel. Sending Maddalena on an errand of mercy to Queen Catherine could be considered treason. Mabel would hang. Surely the worst they would do to a Venetian would be to extradite her. "It is only my business. I am needed to complete the new queen's wardrobe. I must go." She immediately regretted using Lady Anne as an excuse. The tick in the sheriff's eye told her she had made a mistake. "I demand that you inform the Venetian embassy."

"Why, you insolent girl, you cannot demand anything!" He grabbed her arm.

"Let go of me, you big oaf!" Maddalena pushed against him, jerking her arm free.

She was horrified to see the sheriff draw back his hand. She squeezed her eyes shut and squared her stance, bracing for the blow.

When it didn't come, she peered through half-open lids. The sheriff's arm was in the firm grasp of the Duke of Richmond.

There was a scramble of shuffling bodies as the sheriff and the soldiers bowed.

"Your Grace," Maddalena muttered. She curtsied.

"What is the meaning of this?" he asked with more authority than she had seen him use before.

Fumbling for words, the sheriff said, "We are questioning this woman as to her involvement in the murder of one Rose Styles."

"And just when is this little slip of a girl supposed to have murdered one Rose Styles?" the duke asked. He crossed his arms and frowned. Had the situation not been so serious, Maddalena would have burst out laughing.

"They were both missing from Windsor yesterday, Sire. And she was on the same road as the deceased."

"Hmm," the young duke said. "That was obviously an impostor. This Maddalena, or Margaret, as you erroneously call her, was with me."

"Sire?" the sheriff asked.

Maddalena was astonished. "Your Grace?"

"Now be gone with you, and look for a real murderer," he said, waving his hand in dismissal. After they had bowed and shuffled away, he grinned at her. "Now, I'm afraid that tongues will wag a bit, Maddalena. But I would hate to see you hang. I have so few people that I call true friends."

"But Your Grace, you—"

"I know you well enough to know that you are not a murderer. Allow me to use what little influence I have while I still have it."

"Thank you, Your Grace. You are correct. Her friend Thom Bell, an escapee, is quite a better suspect than I."

"Scoundrels always pay, if not to the hangman, certainly to God, Maddalena. If he returns to Windsor, he will get his due."

Maddalena felt a shiver travel up her spine. *If he returns to Windsor?* The thought of ever seeing Thom Bell again made her blood run cold. Surely he would go where he was unknown.

Or will he?

12

Cabot Falls, Vermont
Present Day

$\mathcal{B}$ack home, Sofia shoved aside thoughts about the dark SUV, convincing herself that she had successfully discouraged the stalker from harassing them. Jim would call her bold act of chasing after him foolish, but she felt better that she had tried to confront him. *Il cuor non spaglia.* The literal English translation meant, "The heart sees farther than the head." In other words, "Trust your instincts."

Sofia dialed Officer Quimby's direct line. "Do you have any leads on our stalker yet?" she asked, crossing the fingers of her free hand.

"I'm afraid the only clear prints on the note were yours. But the tread on the street is from a 2005 Chevy Tahoe. It has been plugged twice."

"Plugged?"

"Patched, probably nail holes. Maybe the driver was around a construction site or just unlucky. But there's no way to use the information unless we happen on the vehicle in some criminal act."

She told him about chasing the SUV earlier.

"That is not very wise, ma'am. What would you have done if you caught up to it?"

"I could have at least gotten the license number. I wasn't going to confront the driver. I'll leave the heroics to you." Truthfully, she didn't know what she'd have done. Her adrenaline had been pumping full force at the time.

Disappointed, Sofia decided to research until it was time to pick up Matthew. As she waited for the water to boil for tea, she double-checked her family's schedule. Vanessa had debate practice after school. Wynter was staying late to help decorate the haunted house. Luke had band practice. Jim would get them all home safe and sound. Only Matthew would go with her to the pumpkin patch.

This was not quite how she had envisioned family life. They had grown up so fast. Another year and Vanessa would be college-bound, and then she'd lose one of them about every other year after that. Sighing wistfully, she took her tea and settled down in her favorite chair to see if she could get a better handle on Maddalena Vitari before she became any more morose about time marching on.

She read that Henry VIII was a clotheshorse. He wasn't always an obese, treacherous tyrant. Historians described him as six feet two and strikingly handsome. He wrote plays, performing in them for the entertainment of his court. Some historians believed that he wrote *Greensleeves*, although an Italian applied for the copyright decades later.

How did the epitome of a Renaissance man become such a monster? Maybe if she understood Henry's descent into evil, she could understand how some mother's child grew up to try and terrorize the Parker family.

After a few hours of reading, Sofia poured hot cocoa into a small thermos, packed a peanut butter-and-banana sandwich into an insulated bag, and left Fergus to guard the house.

The school bell rang as she pulled into the pickup circle. Moments later, the double doors burst open and the Cabot Falls munchkins poured out, whooping and jostling one another as they scattered toward the waiting vehicles.

Matthew galloped through the crowd of boisterous free spirits, swung open the door, tossed his backpack onto the floor, and plopped into the front seat, clicking his seat belt. He eagerly accepted the lunch box and left a half-moon gap in the center of the sandwich triangle before speaking. "Thanks, Mom. I needed this." He unscrewed the top on the thermos. "This too."

Sofia circled around a forest-green Toyota and eased into the street. She checked her rearview mirror. Satisfied that there was no dark SUV following her, she relaxed on the short drive.

They arrived at their destination and saw long rows of pumpkins of every size and shade stretching across the field. She parked along the lane and stood for a moment, looking at the sea of orange across the road. Matthew jumped up and down beside her. She grabbed his hand, and together they crossed the street.

They selected a wagon, and a teen boy in a khaki jacket fell in behind them as they wandered the rows. Sofa used her tape measure to find two pumpkins with a circumference large enough to conceal her slow cookers.

"Okay, Matthew, it's your turn to pick the pumpkin for the house. Just remember, it can't be bigger than the stoop, and it should have a good surface to carve. And," she added, "we'll need to be able to lift it, so don't get carried away."

Matthew took a good fifteen minutes deciding between two nearly identical pumpkins. After she paid, one of the employees loaded their pumpkins into the back of the Suburban. Sofia was about to slide into the driver's seat when a dark blue Tahoe pulled into the vacated parking space behind her.

"That's it!" Sofia exclaimed. She stalked back to the SUV and pounded on the driver's-side door window. "You! I'm calling the police right now!"

The window rolled down, and Sofia was face-to-face with a

startled young woman. She could see an infant seat strapped in the rear passenger seat.

"Am I too close?" the young woman asked.

Sofia squeezed her eyes shut. "I'm so sorry. I thought you were somebody else. Please forgive me."

She quickly got behind the wheel of the Suburban, shut the door, and buried her face in her hands. Her shoulders shook as sobs erupted.

"Are you all right, Mom?" Matthew asked. His voice sounded shaky and concerned.

She quickly straightened up, took a deep breath, and inserted her key. The motor hummed to life. "I will be."

The two of them drove home in silence. She had scared that poor young woman, and she had upset her son. She couldn't go on like this. She needed answers, and she needed them soon.

Windsor, England
Spring 1533

Maddalena wondered if the young duke's intervention really put an end to the accusations against her. She was grateful, of course. They would not question the integrity of the king's son.

Still, she swallowed hard, imagining a noose tightening around her neck. She was glad that it hadn't come to a situation where her loyalty to Mabel had to be tested against her desire to survive. Would Mabel have come forward to save her, or was the fear of death too strong?

The circumstances had brought about other complications,

though. By saying that she was with him, the young duke had inadvertently not only sullied her reputation but drawn her closer into the royal circle—a dangerous place to be.

Perhaps most of Queen Catherine's twenty-four years with the king had been ones of privilege, but now she was isolated from her home, friends, and even her daughter. She was forbidden visitors, news from the outside, and even a healthy place in which to spend her last years. Yes, the queen had had a choice. She could have acquiesced to the king's wishes. However, in the hope that one day their daughter, Mary, would inherit the throne, she'd refused. As her punishment, she had been exiled to that mosquito-infested swamp where snakes, frogs, and unspeakable vermin threatened her health.

Maddalena wondered what would happen to the young Duke of Richmond. The king held him in reserve, like an extra horse. He had a privileged life to all appearances. Yet his words haunted her thoughts: *"I may as well use the influence I have while I still have it."* Were his days numbered? If soon-to-be Queen Anne presented the king with a son, what would become of young Henry? And what would become of Maddalena if she were linked to him, even erroneously?

The two of them might have been from different worlds, but they had in common fathers who did not care a thistle's worth for them. She let her breath out in a slow, wistful sigh. She dared not deny that she had been with the duke. That would be akin to calling him a liar. To do so would alienate the duke while opening her up as a suspect once more. Then she and Mabel would face questions they would be better off not answering.

As the coronation of Lady Anne drew near, Maddalena endured the glances and outright stares of the other seamstresses as they feverishly worked to complete the clothes for the coronation they would not themselves witness. At the same time, they created a royal layette.

After the coronation, the couple, accompanied by great numbers of servants, took a hunting trip. Then they settled in Greenwich to await the birth. It was to King Henry's great disappointment that Anne birthed a daughter on September 7. She was as ginger-haired as the king and the duke. He named her Elizabeth—the same as the duke's mother and the same as Henry's own mother.

As another damp, cold winter approached, Maddalena remained in the clutches of the king's service without any word from Allessandro. New bolts of fabric arrived in the vault. If they were from her father's visit to the court, she was not privy to it. He made no effort to see her. Yet she still she held hope for a life with Allessandro. She wrote often.

> *Allessandro, cara mia, have you forgotten me? Time rolls on, and I fear that I shall never see you again. I try to imagine what you look like now, but alas, you are frozen in time, and you look just as you did when I last saw you on the dock. So much has happened that I want to tell you. I paint when I can, and I sketch a good deal. The royal painter Hans Holbein is quite encouraging. I strive to take his advice, which is to stay in the shadows and make everyone look beautiful. It is more difficult than I thought to do either. My heart belongs to you now and forever.*

She handed over her sealed letter to Alice to slip into the diplomatic pouch on its way to Italy. It took much faith, knowing that its fate was out of her hands.

Maddalena wrapped her cloak around her shoulders and stepped from the portico and into the brisk October wind. The ground was already hard beneath her feet as she trudged along the side of the road toward the farmhouse just outside Windsor. The woman who lived there was especially talented at tatting, and Mabel sometimes paid her for special designs to edge sleeve cuffs.

The wind had picked up, and Maddalena had to face into it returning to the castle. With her head down, she very nearly ran into the duke as he prepared to mount an ebony jennet. He was without humor on this gray day.

"Are you all right, Your Grace?" Maddalena asked. "I have not seen you of late."

"My hours of study have increased. Things are changing. You will hear of it soon enough." With that, he mounted and urged the horse forward.

Maddalena watched his image grow smaller and then disappear. He seemed so unhappy. His teasing smile had completely disappeared. *Curious.* It seemed his father's interest in him had not lessened. She could understand how that would weigh heavily on him. It was not an enviable position in which to be.

After she stowed the lace in the fabric vault, she returned to the sewing room.

"We have been told to ready a wardrobe for the duke's marriage," Mabel said. "We have less than three weeks to complete it."

"The duke?" Maddalena asked. "Which duke?"

"Your duke," Lucy said. She laughed hysterically.

"But he's so young. He has not reached his majority," she protested. So that was why he seemed so sad. "To whom?"

"Lady Mary Howard," Mabel replied. "We will not be concerned with a dress for her."

Maddalena understood now. The Howards were politically powerful and wealthy. And they were cousins of Queen Anne. She was tightening her grasp on the crown. But the king was no less motivated. His popularity and his power in the country were in jeopardy because of his marriage in defiance of the Church. He no doubt needed both the infusion of wealth from the Howard dowry and their influence. He was sacrificing his son to achieve it.

"Margaret, bring the bobbin of Venetian lace with the rose pattern from the vault, and be quick about it." Mabel turned her attention back to the cut velvet sleeve she was working on.

The gray day had darkened to charcoal, a signal that rain was not far behind. Maddalena realized that she should have brought a light, as the vault was heavy with shadows and the newly acquired bolts of fabric leaned against one another at precarious angles, looking ready to fall at any moment. She gingerly stepped around the first few. The bobbin of lace would be right behind them if no one had moved it in her absence.

From the corner of her eye, she glimpsed a slight movement. Startled, she stepped back. Was a bolt about to fall? The shadow shifted. "Hello? Is someone there? You are not supposed to be in here." She paused, cocking her head to listen. "Who's there?"

She felt goose bumps crawl up her spine and tickle her neck as one shadow separated from the rest and revealed itself as that of a man. The dim light reflected on something, and she could see the distinct silhouette of a knife.

Maddalena gasped. "Thom Bell!"

How could she fend him off with only her fists?

13

Cabot Falls, Vermont
Present Day

Sofia punched down the bread dough, probably with more force than she needed. She was still angry with herself for her behavior at the pumpkin patch. That poor woman must've thought she was insane.

Maybe she was at that moment. What if it had been the stalker? What would she have done? Scold him like a naughty child? She hadn't even considered Matthew at the time; he saw it all! She'd never been so irresponsible in her life.

Sofia floured the board and slapped the dough onto it, kneading it and shaping it into a long loaf to rise again. The cold weather always put her in the mood for soup, salad, and garlic bread for supper. It wouldn't take too long to finish when she returned.

She called to Jim that she'd be back in a jiff as she slipped on her jacket and grabbed her purse and keys. The aunts would arrive tomorrow with the costumes. Aunt Louisa had requested lasagna with meat sauce, so naturally, Aunt Rachel wanted vegetable lasagna.

The rearview mirror cast a bright light in her eyes and when she came to a stop at a traffic signal, she adjusted it. As she did, she caught the reflection of a dark SUV behind her. It had a red sticker in the lower right corner of the windshield. Sofia turned into the grocer's parking lot and let out a sigh as the SUV continued down the street. *I've got to stop being so paranoid,* she told herself.

Her boots clicked against the pavement as she double-timed it to the entrance. The doors swung open automatically, and she hastily made her purchases and left the store. She hurried toward the Suburban but came to a quick stop as she felt the blood drain from her face. The dark SUV with a red sticker in the lower corner of the windshield was in the parking lot. It was empty. The driver must have doubled back and followed her inside.

Sofia's first instinct was to get out of there before he returned. She ignored that impulse and went for plan B. She shoved her groceries onto the front seat, grabbed her grocery list and pencil from her purse, and approached the SUV. She quickly jotted down the license plate number.

Officer Quimby had said the tire tread he'd captured was from the passenger-side rear tire. Hunkering down, she hastily made a rubbing of the tread while intermittently glancing toward the exit to be sure the driver wasn't coming out. She was about to leave when she spotted papers on the seat. A quick pull at the door handle showed it was unlocked. The inside flooded with light as she flung the door open.

Hurriedly she pulled the papers to her. It was an auto rental agreement from Montpelier. The name on the paper was Sam Borasino. She'd never heard of him. She closed the door, plunging the interior once again into shadow. Dodging behind the next car, she saw a lone man exit the store and pause to tug a suede safari hat brim low over his eyes. He was a big man, and his frame seemed to block the light from inside. He was holding a plastic cup from the deli. A wisp of steam curled upward and vanished in the cold air.

Sofia let out her breath in relief. He'd gone in for coffee or maybe hot cocoa. This probably wasn't even the same SUV. Yet how many of them would have red stickers like that?

The man jammed his free hand into the pocket of a

khaki-colored trench coat and trotted in her direction. But instead of going directly to his vehicle, he walked straight to her Suburban, cupping his eyes to peer inside. She held her breath, watching until he finally slid behind the wheel of his own rental. He made no move to leave, but kept his face aimed at the exit door.

She turned her jacket collar up; then, stepping into the middle of a family that was heading into the store, she slipped back inside. There was no point in calling the police. There was no law against parking in the lot while finishing his coffee. If she ever wanted the police to take her fears seriously, she'd need more proof. Sofia gathered her courage and exited the store. She strolled to her car without looking in his direction and drove out with her uninvited escort close behind.

Sofia pulled in front of the police station and parked. She watched in her side mirror until the SUV passed. Then she grabbed her purse and the rubbing and went inside. "Do you have an evidence envelope I can put this in?" she asked the desk attendant.

He raised an eyebrow. "Evidence envelope? And you are . . . ?"

"Leaving this for Officer Quimby," she finished. "He'll know what to do with it."

The chair squeaked as the heavyset officer grunted and pulled a bag from the bottom drawer of his desk. "Fill in the blanks, and I'll date, time-stamp, and initial the receipt."

Sofia hastily filled in the information, omitting Borasino's name. Then she thanked the officer and headed home. She had the stalker's name now. And she had the license plate number. Perhaps it wasn't the wisest decision she'd ever made, but she decided to follow up on Borasino on her own before telling Officer Quimby. She needed to know why this man had inserted himself into their lives.

It was what she had seen on the seat next to the rental paper that made her want to know more. It was a box of ammunition labeled *20-Count 9mm Cartridges.*

Where there was ammunition, there would undoubtedly be a gun.

What exactly was he up to?

Windsor, England
Autumn 1533

Maddalena stared in horror at the figure that had emerged from the shadows. Her worst fear materialized. Thom Bell loomed before her, brandishing a knife. She froze in terror. She had her scissors, but if she was close enough to injure him, he would be close enough to stab her.

"You little guttersnipe!" he hissed like a snake about to strike. "You got the whole countryside out lookin' for me. I'll silence that mouth of yours once and for eternity." He took a step forward.

"Stop! Don't come any closer!" She tried to scream, but she managed only to croak like a frog. She took a step back, nearly losing her balance as her foot struck the base of a bolt of fabric. It shifted slightly. She flourished the scissors. "I'm not afraid of you, you coward!" she lied.

Mentally she was trying to calculate how far she was far from the door. Could she turn and flee into the hall before he reached her? Before he could plunge a knife into her heart or slit her throat? And if she could, was there anyone in the corridor to help? Women's clothes were so cumbersome, it was difficult enough to maneuver, let alone run. Perhaps if she could keep him talking, appeal to his high opinion of himself, she could stall until someone came.

"They would never believe you'd come back here, Thom. They are probably scouring the woods for you. And who would have believed you could escape prison? They must have been surprised to find you gone."

He sniggered. "Everyone has a price, some cheaper than others. We even had a few ha'pennies left over, Rose and me did."

"She loved you enough to steal my money and use all of her own to get you out of there," Maddalena said. She edged back ever so stealthily, just a half step. "Why did you kill her?" She slid her foot back a half step more. "You did kill her, didn't you?"

"That strumpet was like a boulder on me back. Always complainin'. Always wantin' something," he said. "All you wenches are the same. And don't take another step back. You are just delaying your death. Give me trouble, and I'll make it slow and painful, I will." He shifted his weight, a signal that he was about to spring.

Maddalena braced herself. In a flash, he sprang, and at the same instant, she shoved the nearest bolt of fabric with her shoulder. Like dominoes, each was propelled into the next and tumbled, knocking Thom off his feet and pinning him beneath the heavy load.

At last Maddalena found her voice. "Help! Help! Murderer!"

There was a stampede of feet in the hall. Mabel, Alice, Lucy, and Joan rushed in only to come to a quick halt, staring. Suddenly, Lucy cackled and flung herself on top of the bolts, bouncing as if she were riding a horse. The others joined her, piling on top.

"Well, don't stand there gaping, Margaret," Mabel said. "Find the nearest guards and bring them here before we use our cording to hang him ourselves."

Maddalena, relieved beyond belief, spun around and raced

down the hall, breathlessly calling to the two palace guards at the far end.

The gray clouds parted like curtains opening on a play. By noon, the sky was blue except for the wispy white clouds. The fair weather brought the young nobles to the courtyard to wage their mock battles, and the young ladies of leisure soon followed to cheer them on. Their laughter floated up to the sewing room.

Mabel looked up. "Margaret, you had a harrowing experience this morning, and your hand is still shaking. Why don't you take your sketchbook and go out until you steady yourself?"

Maddalena was surprised by the sudden show of kindness. Or maybe it was gratitude because she had kept Mabel's confidence. "I am quite—"

Mabel's raised eyebrow signaled her to accept the offer in the spirit it was given.

"Yes. Thank you, mum." Could it be that the incident with Thom Bell marked a change in the tide? Would the others also now accept her without hostility?

Maddalena, attracted to the giggling and whispers of the noble ladies, strolled closer to a gathered crowd. She climbed atop a pylon so that she could see above their heads.

From there she could see broadswords slash through the air and then make contact with a loud clank. Over and over, from right to left and left to right, the two mock warriors swung their weapons.

She smiled. *They are boys playing at being men with broad-swords only three-fourths the size of those early knights' weapons displayed in the great hall.* Yet one wrong move, one strike in anger, and the swords could cause real damage.

The two boys at the center of attention were the young dukes, Richmond and Howard—childhood friends who would soon be brothers-in-law. Henry Howard was a little older than Henry Fitzroy and perhaps a bit stronger, although the king's son had inherited his father's height. She cocked her head, comparing the two. She could definitely say from an artist's point of view that the king's son was more striking, even with the net cap covering his glorious ginger hair. His features seemed a fortuitous combination of his parents, the best of each.

With his tunic removed and his silk garment open to his waist, he looked more in his element than in the stuffy, boxy wardrobe of the day.

Watching the proceedings were Queen Anne, her ladies-in-waiting, and a few who had accompanied state visitors. Anne was Howard's cousin and Richmond's stepmother now. Soon she would add aunt to her ties to the throne. She was stone-faced as she watched the two duel. What was she thinking at that moment? One miscalculated blow to her stepson's head and her daughter would be heir to the throne?

Maddalena noticed that some of the ladies were glancing toward the upper building. She followed their gazes to the balcony where King Henry stood looking down on the duel. His expression was as much an enigma as his queen's. Maddalena wondered if the king looked at the handsome young man as his son to be cherished or as his rival for the throne. Surely it had not escaped his attention that Henry Fitzroy was popular with the people while the king was more loathed by the day.

The sword master diplomatically declared it a draw, and the two combatants bowed and shook hands.

By then, Maddalena had made a hasty sketch of her friend,

skin glistening with the dew of sweat. She closed her book as she saw him approach and hopped down from the pylon to curtsy.

"I was sharp with you the other day, Maddalena. I apologize. I was upset, but it was not your doing," he told her.

"About the marriage?" she asked.

The young duke winced, and Maddalena remembered she was not talking to her equal but to royalty.

She dropped her eyes. "It is my time to apologize. I should not pry."

"It's because you genuinely care, I feel sure. Yes, it is the marriage. I must do what I must, but I do not have to like it." He glanced around. "She's rather a stick-in-the-mud."

Maddalena giggled. "Shush. Someone will hear."

His mouth split into the familiar mischievous grin she so admired. "Well, at least we won't have to spend time with each other. I daresay she doesn't care for me much either."

"No, Your Grace?" Maddalena couldn't imagine anyone not liking this spirited boy. "I don't understand."

"The king has his reasons, I'm sure. Perhaps his queen will give him a son the next time." He paused. "Meanwhile, I am held in reserve as heir, just as he once was. The difference is he wants me better prepared for it than he was. I study history, diplomacy, government, geography, and war strategy. King Henry VII, my grandfather, saw that Uncle Arthur had these qualities. But my father studied art, literature, music, and dance. None of these prepared him to run a country or recognize when he was being manipulated by connivers. He doesn't want that for me."

Maddalena could offer no solace to her friend. She watched as he walked away, shoulders squared as he no doubt had been taught and wearing the mask he showed everyone but her. He was to marry a stranger he didn't love, as she could not marry the one she loved. Would either of them ever find happiness?

Back in the sewing room, her heart was burdened by the young duke's woes. However, she felt the invisible wall had crumbled between herself and the ladies who had aided her against Thom Bell. She felt hopeful that life would be more tolerable.

Tolerable? She wryly laughed out loud.

14

Cabot Falls, Vermont
Present Day

Sofia nearly burst out laughing at the anxious expressions on the faces of her family. "Come on, people, it's not that late. Supper will be ready in an hour."

"Can I help?" Jim asked, taking the grocery bag from her hand. "The kids have already set the table, but we didn't know what else to do."

"It won't speed up supper, if that's your motive. But yes, wash the endive and chop it into bite-size pieces while I get the bread into the oven." Sofia turned her attention to her kids, who were waiting for tasks. "Is your homework done?" At their halfhearted responses, she shooed them out of the kitchen.

"Are you going to tell me what happened?" Jim asked once the kids were out of earshot.

Sofia dropped meatballs into the broth and lowered the temperature. "How did you know?"

"We weren't married only yesterday, sweetheart. I knew the moment you walked in the door. The mysterious SUV again?"

"Yes, but I think it'll soon be over." She retrieved the vegetables she had prepared earlier in the day and stirred them into the soup while Jim scraped the chopped endive into the salad bowl. "Officer Quimby has some new evidence he'll follow up on." She didn't like holding back information from Jim. But she wanted to have all the information before sharing. "The aunts are coming tomorrow," she said to change the subject.

Jim wasn't taking the bait. Sofia knew his silence meant he wanted more.

"Nothing beats soup, salad, and fresh-baked bread, right?" she asked, trying again to divert the conversation.

"Not having a stalker would beat it," he replied, pulling her close so that she could smell his aftershave. He wrapped both arms around her.

"Oh, gross," Vanessa said as she walked in. "Parents! Not in front of the children, please."

Jim laughed. "Then go in the other room because I'm about to plant a big kiss on your mom."

"Ewww!" Vanessa scurried out.

The next morning, Sofia rose early. She prepared two lasagnas, stowed them in the fridge, and then hurried to the basement to use the computer before the family got up. She searched Sam Borasino and Montpelier, the only personal information she had gleaned in her short reconnaissance. A list appeared: Samuel G. Borasino, Samuel E. Borasino, and Sam G. Borasino Jr.

She printed out the addresses and phone numbers. "Which one of you is the mysterious and persistent stalker? Whichever one, it's my turn now."

She closed her eyes, calling on her memory. Was there an initial on the agreement? Was there a Jr. on the signature? She couldn't recall either. If only she'd had more time to read it. Something about the guy made her think that he was not a young man. That didn't mean he wasn't a junior, though. And that was the only Sam. On a whim, she dialed the Sam Jr.'s number.

A woman answered and said that Sam was out of town on business. *What kind of business?* Sofia wondered. She searched for businesses associated with the name Sam G. Borasino Jr. One listing appeared, and Sofia leaned back in the chair, staring in disbelief: Sam G. Borasino, Detective Agency.

The agency website included a biography: A former Green Beret and NYC cop, Borasino retired to Montpelier, Vermont, where he conducted private detective work. The photo was the first clear look she'd had of him. He was clean-shaven and graying with a slightly modified military haircut. His face was a map of the things he must have seen. But he looked fit, with his shoulders still straight. The article said that he maintained the morning habit of running.

What did he want with them? It had to be a mistake. Of all the people in Cabot Falls, the Parker family was the least likely to be in trouble.

Was it a mistake to have left the license number and tread rubbing for Quimby? For a moment she thought about getting it back before he checked in. But she decided she'd done the right thing. After all, they were law-abiding people. It was clearly a case of mistaken identity, which the detective would soon find out.

"Sofia?" Jim called from the main floor. "Coffee's on."

Sofia dressed her face in a smile and hurried up the stairs. Maybe a cup of coffee with Jim would jump-start her groggy brain cells and she'd come up with some logical answers. The kids would sleep in, and maybe she'd make pancakes. The aunts were only an hour away, and if she knew Aunt Louisa, she was already chiding Rachel that they were "burning daylight," as she often said.

Sofia's hunch had been right. She'd just put away the griddle when she heard Aunt Rachel's gravelly voice outside the front door:

"Louisa, you should have been a race car driver. I'm surprised we didn't wind up wrapped around a tree."

"Well you'd lose a race with a snail, Rachel," Aunt Louisa's unmistakable voice replied. "It's dangerous to go slow. The rest of them would run over us."

No one could chase away worries like those two wonderful old gals. And right now, Sofia was more angry than worried that a man connected to law enforcement was terrifying her family. She truly hoped never to see him again.

Windsor, England
Winter 1535

Maddalena had seen only glimpses of Henry Fitzroy after that morning now two years past. He lived in London and visited Windsor only when summoned. The king had traded him off to the powerful Howards in return for their influence and Mary Howard's impressive dowry. Was the king truly preparing him to be the legitimate heir over his half sisters, Mary and Elizabeth? Or did King Henry think that if he kept his son out of sight, the commoners would forget how much they loved him and disliked his father?

Elizabeth, the result of Queen Anne's only successful child-birth, had grown into a feisty little toddler, padding down corridors with her adoring but exhausted nanny chasing after her. The royal couple paid little attention to her as they had turned to displays of bickering, the king growing more irascible each day. As he stormed through the corridors, servants scattered in every direction, disappearing into stairwells or rooms until he had vented his ire and passed by, hobbling on the painful leg that had never healed after the jousting incident.

Maddalena left her childhood behind as she continued to work in the king's service to earn enough wages to pay her way home. The gossipmongers said that the king was anxious because he still had no legitimate male heir, as he had not yet taken the final step to legitimize the duke. The king made little effort to hide the fact that he distrusted Anne. She became more adamant in her Calvinistic beliefs and chastised him for his tax war on the churches while still demanding more material things.

Queen Anne did not hide her displeasure, and she unleashed it on the king and the subjects. The people still hurled insults at her in the streets so that she rarely left the confines of the palace.

There were whispers, too, that Queen Catherine was failing in health and might not see this Candlemas. It made Maddalena sad to think of the ailing woman in that forsaken swamp, dying with no one but her servant at her side.

The king seemed oblivious to her plight, however, and continued his plans to have an extravagant Christmas, pageants and all. He brought the Duke of Richmond and his half sister Mary Tudor to the palace, no doubt to show the state visitors that England was still paradise on earth and the monarchy was one big happy family.

All this was on Maddalena's mind as she hurried with Alice toward the castle to face the day's work. "The innkeeper's son has asked my permission to marry you," Alice told her. "Your year's wages will do as a dowry." Alice's eyes danced in that wild, unfocused way that signaled her ever-loosening grasp on reality.

Maddalena stopped walking and stared, open-mouthed, before speaking. "Alice, you are not my mother. You have no right to give permission to anyone regarding me," she said, her patience waning. She was grateful for the woman's support since she'd been cast away by her own flesh and blood. Truly, she would do anything she could for the old woman. Anything but pretend she was Alice's daughter and marry that oaf.

"But I told him he could—"

"Then you can tell him he cannot," Maddalena said as firmly as she could. "Alice, I will spend my days in a convent before I will marry anyone but Allessandro. Tell me that you understand me. I want to hear you say it."

Alice smiled at her. "You have so much to learn, Lily." She shook her head. "So very much. But I take care of my own."

Maddalena threw up her hands in frustration as they entered the sewing room. She dropped the subject for the time being, but somehow she had to get through to the poor thing. How much longer could Alice continue to work? And what would happen to her when she no longer could? Perhaps that was what motivated her to act on Maddalena's behalf, no matter how wrong she was.

Now Maddalena was grateful to spend most of her days in the sewing room with the others, creating the ever-expanding wardrobe of the royal couple as they strove to remain the enviable fashion trendsetters. But soon she would be paid her annual wage and she would have enough to buy her way to Venice. She would see for herself if Allessandro had waited for her. It was difficult to remain sure when she'd had no word from him over these past few years.

She was sewing fox fur to a cloak of dark red velvet when Lady Jane Seymour stepped into the room. Maddalena might not have known her, except for the palace wags whispering about her and the king during Anne's absences. "Margaret Vitari is requested in the chambers of Queen Anne. I will show her the way."

"I know the way, milady" Maddalena said, her voice barely audible. "You needn't wait." She dreaded being in Anne's presence when the air was permeated with anxiety and anger.

When she arrived in the apartments of the queen, she saw that there was no trace of what once had been. Most of the furniture was now French and royal blue. Anne looked up from her needlepoint. "Well, don't just gape. Come in and listen carefully. I want pearls across the bodice—lots of them. Rows and rows of pearls. And I want ermine on the sleeves. I—"

The door to the apartments burst open, and King Henry strode in. Maddalena was sure that her own expression mirrored the alarm on the queen's face. Henry was in a rage as she'd never seen him.

"You witch! You sorceress!" he roared. "My advisors were right. You are indeed from the devil!" The king paced in front of her. "Oh, my poor children! They lie in their beds, writhing in pain." He turned and pointed an accusing finger at her. "Poison! You—you plied your witchcraft on them!"

"I—" Anne held up her hands, palms forward as if to ward off his words.

"What witch's brew did you give my children and for what purpose? And do not deny your dalliances, woman. Did you think that they would not reach the king's ears?"

"Not true!" Anne protested.

"You call the king a liar? Sorceresses burn at the stake on earth, and then they burn in the eternal fire of damnation! You will pay for your treachery, Anne!" The king spun on his heel and stormed from the room, slamming the heavy door behind him.

Maddalena stared at the woman, who slumped into a tufted French parlor chair. Her expression was a mix of fear and bewilderment, and she was pale, as if the blood had drained from her body. The room fell silent for what seemed like an eternity.

Finally, Maddalena dared speak. "Should I come back another time, Your Grace? I can return later, if you wish." After that scene, she wondered if the queen would even be there later. Or would she be hauled off to some dungeon or even prison like a common criminal? From the sound of King Henry, he planned worse than exile.

Dismissed and stunned, Maddalena returned to the sewing room, sworn to secrecy about the event she had witnessed. She passed along Queen Anne's instructions and sat down to sketch out a more lavish wardrobe for King Henry. It would do Anne no good to appear more elegant than he—that is, if she was still in public view, all things considered.

The festivities went as scheduled, and unless the state visitors were privy to the rumors, they knew nothing of the intrigue in the depths of the court. Queen Anne looked radiant in her royal blue and sparkling white pearls. Maddalena had applied lace with a flower motif, its blooms mimicking hundreds of little pearls.

Mary Tudor and Henry, Duke of Richmond and Somerset, recovered in time to attend all of the events, and Maddalena felt sure that the king had by now assumed they merely fell ill coincidentally. By all appearances, he was attentive to Queen Anne.

The duke visited with his mother, Lady Elizabeth Clinton, née Blount, in his grandparents' apartment at Windsor before he was to return to St. James Castle in London, the home of the Howards.

Maddalena was entering the palace as the duke stood at his carriage and bade them goodbye. Their eyes met, and she nodded. He acknowledged her with a wink, but there was no friendly smile. He looked drawn, tired, and resigned.

And Mary Tudor was returned to exile without being allowed to visit her dying mother.

The castle was again in turmoil. With the festivities over, King Henry met daily with his council, preparing a case against Anne. There seemed little reason to celebrate the New Year. Yet the aroma of roast ducks, a gift from the king to his subjects in

Windsor, permeated the rows of inns and taverns that lined the Thames. Once a year they ate like kings.

The boisterous sounds of celebration filled the air. Maddalena and Alice left the chill of their own room and hurried across the alley to the King's Arms Inn.

Inside it was as warm as it was noisy. Flames leaped and danced around the heavy kettles hanging in the high fireplace. They bubbled with boiled root vegetables brought up from the cellar. A woman slowly rotated the roast on a spit. The aroma of melted duck fat was nearly overwhelming, although it was only a strong second to the nose-stinging smell of ale.

The population of Windsor had expanded with the influx of country dwellers for a free meal, compliments of the king they never saw. To them he must have seemed a benevolent man. A young man with golden hair curled about his ears and wearing a billed cap like she'd seen on visitors to the palace stood near the hearth, strumming on a stringed instrument and singing. His voice barely carried above the noise of the revelers:

> *Good Catherine lay dying,*
> *Ne'er seen anywhere.*
> *The king says to Anne*
> *I wish you were there.*

Maddalena gasped. "Alice, we should go. What he sings is treason. We shouldn't be in here. Besides, the people are all but out of control." There were men in soldiers' uniforms and peasant linen and women in wool tunics with halos of leaves around their heads. And they all seemed beyond fear of retribution.

A heavyset man with an eye patch laughed heartily and slammed his pewter tankard against the long bench. "Ale, girl! I am empty!" Ale streaked his scraggly beard, and a time-whitened scar protruded from under his patch, down his cheek and up across his forehead. He grinned at the serving maid refilling his tankard, revealing a row of yellowed teeth.

Alice grabbed Maddalena's hand and pulled her toward a bench opposite the one-eyed man. "We will have our first good meal since the king married that woman. Sit. It is his life the minstrel risks, not ours."

Maddalena was not so sure about that. But the lure of hot, succulent meat instead of bread soaked in milk and honey was too tempting to refuse. Besides, soon she would have enough money to buy her way to Venice—and to Allessandro, if he still waited for her.

The one-eyed man tapped his eye patch. "Scares you, does it? Lost me eye to the end of a Spaniard's spear in Henry's war." He narrowed his eye and studied Maddalena. "Dark eyes, dark hair, olive skin. Are you a Spanish lass?"

"I am Venetian," Maddalena replied. She said it with less conviction than in years past. Despite all the merriment that surrounded her, she could not help but feel that a shroud of doom would descend upon them at any moment. Somewhere in her brain, a small voice whispered, *England is not through with you yet, Maddalena Vitari.*

15

Cabot Falls, Vermont
Present Day

That voice in her head whispering dire warnings had subsided. Sofia realized that she was actually humming as she put the two lasagnas into the oven and set the timer.

She could hear the whir of the portable sewing machines her aunts had set up in the dining room, followed by the squeals of joy from her daughters as they tried on their dresses.

Vanessa and Wynter ran into the kitchen, both in their Renaissance costumes in rich brocade. The dresses were different in design, of course. The aunts knew what it was like to want to be distinct from one's sister. But they both had an overdress style with intricate bodices—Wynter in dark green and Vanessa in pale green. The girls twirled as Sofia admired the beautiful work on her equally beautiful daughters.

The girls ran out of the kitchen and returned a minute later in their dresses for the dance. The underdresses, while appropriate peeking out from beneath the Renaissance costumes, were also thoroughly modern dresses for the school dance.

"You girls look like you should be on the red carpet," Sofia said.

Vanessa turned to Wynter and mimed talking into a microphone. "Who are you wearing?"

Wynter struck a pose. "This was designed exclusively for me by The Aunts." She flipped her hair, struck another pose, and strolled out of the room. Sofia could hear her back in the dining room, the aunts fussing over her again.

Vanessa stayed in the kitchen. "Thanks, Mom."

"Don't thank me. All I did was make a phone call."

"Well, I'm sorry if I made a face when you told me I was getting a homemade dress for the dance. I love it. I feel really lucky." Vanessa gave Sofia a quick hug and padded out of the kitchen.

Sofia took a moment to solidify that moment in her memory.

After the aunts made final snips of loose threads, they packed up their sewing machines and stowed them in Louisa's car trunk. To Sofia's dismay, they turned their attention to her kitchen.

"Tear the lettuce. You know that knives leave a metallic taste on the lettuce. Tear," Aunt Rachel scolded.

"Observe," Louisa said. "You are so behind the times. This is a ceramic knife, not metal."

Rachel pursed her lips. "Who's behind the times? Does this hairdo say chic, or does it not?"

"It says you don't know you're old. That's what it says," Louisa replied.

Sofia rolled her eyes. People who didn't know them would think they were at odds with each other. Even Jim, who'd known them for decades, fled to his workshop.

After lunch, Sofia stood on the stoop, waving until her aunts' car was out of sight. She had turned to go into the house when she heard Pat Cooper call her name. Her neighbor scuttled toward her with Willow following close behind.

"A man came to our house yesterday, but I didn't want to tell you while you had company. He asked a lot of questions about your family," Pat said. "Things like how long you've lived here and did you live beyond your income." Pat crossed her arms defiantly. "I'm no rat. I sent him packing."

Goose bumps crept up Sofia's arms. She bristled at the thought of someone questioning her neighbor about her. Not that she had secrets. But it was creepy. "Can you describe the man?"

"I can do better than that." Pat reached into her gray cardigan pocket and handed Sofia a business card. "His SUV was parked on the street for a bit. I think he went to the other neighbors too. Not everyone is as discreet as I am, Sofia. You can tell me anything, you know. Are you sure you aren't in some kind of trouble? Maybe one of your children, or—"

"I've got to go, Pat," Sofia said after she saw the name on the card: Sam Borasino, Private Investigator. "Thank you." She spun around and ran inside, slamming the door behind her. "Jim! Jim! Where are you?" She double-timed to the side door and found Jim out in his workshop, sealing the wood on one panel of the booth he was building for the Renaissance Festival.

He grinned. "Coming to supervise?"

She shook her head. "The stalker is a detective. He's been questioning the neighbors about us."

Jim rested the paintbrush across the top of the paint can and slipped off his work gloves. "Whoa. Slow down, honey. How do you know all this? I've only been out here thirty minutes." He pulled up a handmade sawhorse. "Sit."

Sofia plopped onto the sawhorse next to Jim. It was time to tell him everything. She told him how she got Borasino's name from the rental agreement in the SUV, how she looked him up on the Web, and that Pat told her he was questioning the neighbors. "Why is he doing this, Jim? What if it's something bad?"

"What if it is something good?" Jim wrapped his arms around her shoulders. "Sofia, that was a dangerous thing you did. And probably illegal too. But this is good news, right? I mean, he's a private investigator. Borasino must be aboveboard, or Vermont wouldn't have issued him a license to be an investigator. Whatever he's doing, it must be legitimate business. And we have nothing to hide."

Sofia's lips tightened into a thin line as he spoke. She was a basically positive person too. But how could Jim not see that this was wrong? "But the notes. The warnings!"

"What if the notes weren't from Borasino but from someone we haven't even considered?" Jim suggested.

Sofia considered that unsettling possibility.

"Mom! Telephone!" Wynter called.

"I'll call them back," Sofia replied. She wanted time to think about this development more.

"It's that police officer!"

Sofia planted a quick kiss on Jim's cheek and hurried to the phone in the kitchen.

Officer Quimby mostly told her what she already knew. The license plate was for a rental agency in Montpelier.

"Have you compared the tread evidence to his rental?" Sofia asked. She wanted to nail this guy to the threats. "He's been questioning my neighbors too."

"That's what private investigators do, Mrs. Parker."

There was a silence on the other end. Sofia could hear the rustle of papers. "Mrs. Parker, I don't know what the PI is after. But you reported the SUV following your daughter the first time a week ago."

"That's right. And he's dogged us ever since," Sofia said.

"According to the rental agency, Borasino rented the car two days ago. He can't be your stalker."

Sofia felt her lips begin to numb, as if she were going to pass out. She leaned against the counter until the room stopped spinning around her. What could a PI want with them? And if Borasino wasn't the stalker, who was?

Windsor, England
Winter 1536

It was only a week after the celebration of the New Year when word spread among the servants at Windsor that Catherine of Aragon had died at Kimbolton Castle, where she had been transferred from Manor of the More. Maddalena could only imagine how bleak it must have been on that gray January day, surrounded by the desolate swamp.

Even as she lay on her deathbed, Henry refused her permission to visit with her closest friend, Maria de Salinas, or with Mary Tudor. Only Ambassador Chapuys from Spain saw her in her final days.

Defiant until the end, Catherine made a will, leaving to her daughter Mary one of the few possessions she had not sold to sustain herself and her servant. She also dictated a letter to Henry, although no one was privy to its contents.

She received a proper state funeral at Peterborough Cathedral—not as the queen, but as the widow of Henry's brother, Arthur. Neither Henry nor Anne attended.

The faithful still referred to her as Queen Catherine and not the Dowager Princess of Wales, as King Henry preferred. Rumors that Anne had murdered her swept through the crowds after the coroner ruled homicide by slow poison.

Maddalena, with Alice and the other seamstresses, joined the throngs of subjects who went to the chapel to pray for her soul. She wondered how many of them had prayed for her during her tormented exile. But then, how many of them could even imagine what the queen had been through?

Anne's fate seemed only a matter of time. Rumors of her witchcraft, of secret testimonies by witnesses, and Henry's own testimony made the outcome no surprise. Henry even saw that the Duke of Richmond was on the panel to seal her fate. She was declared an adulteress and a sorceress, which usually meant death by fire.

Maddalena didn't believe in witchcraft, but she was not so sure that the queen hadn't tried to poison Mary and the duke as King Henry had accused her. After all, if they were out of the way, Elizabeth would be assured the throne. Anne would be the Queen Mother. That seemed far more inviting than being a mere cousin to Mary and stepmother to Henry Fitzroy.

The following spring, the king ordered that Anne be subjected to a more humane death—beheading rather than being burnt alive. In early May, Maddalena was shocked when she was summoned to the Tower of London, where Anne was being held.

"What is appropriate attire for a beheading?" Anne asked. Her voice was flat, with no trace of bitterness or fear.

"Your Grace?" Maddalena stepped back, gasping in horror.

"I want nothing with a collar that could impede the sword. It must be quick. Henry has promised the best executioner." Her eyes defied her colorless voice. Tears moistened her lashes, yet she remained erect, head high.

"I can't do this, Your Grace. Please don't ask me," Maddalena pleaded. Her instinct said to turn and run, yet she realized she couldn't.

"You must, little one, just as I must move toward the fate God has given me."

"It isn't God," Maddalena blurted out. "It is a . . . a . . . ." She wanted to shout, "It's a madman!" But she dared not. The Tower walls had ears.

"I should perhaps wear dark blue, don't you think? And I'd

like to wear the nice little white French cap. Bring them to me and help me look my best, Margaret."

Maddalena nodded. "When, Your Grace?"

"Soon, I hear. Soon. But I die with the knowledge that my daughter, Elizabeth, will one day wear the crown."

Maddalena curtsied and left, Queen Anne's last words echoing in her mind. How could Anne be so sure that Elizabeth would be chosen over the Duke of Richmond? A woman, even over an illegitimate male, seemed unlikely. Considering the king's changes of mind and heart, who knew what tomorrow would bring?

She thought, as Anne must have, that King Henry might grant clemency to Anne. But three days after her meeting, Maddalena took a royal blue dress with no embellishments to the Tower.

Because Anne was queen, only nobles were allowed to attend, but the square was jammed with the whole bloodthirsty lot of them. They milled about, laughing and enjoying the spectacle as one would enjoy a mummers' play. It was mid-May, and the sun was heavy upon them as Maddalena and one of the queen's ladies walked with the queen to the steps of the platform. "Stay with me, Margaret," she begged, "lest I turn and flee to my own humiliation. Steady my pace so that I faint not."

At the foot of the wooden steps, they paused. Maddalena looked up to see a giant of a man with a black hood covering his face. He held a heavy sword at his side.

Standing next to the block on which Anne would rest her head was the Duke of Richmond. He seemed almost in a trance, pale and expressionless. Anne turned toward Maddalena and said, "Thank you." And then she climbed the steep steps with the aid of her servant. She suddenly seemed terribly small. Anne handed the executioner the customary fee so he would make the strike clean and swift, and then she prayed aloud. "God save the king," she called out.

Anne's servant tied a blindfold over her eyes. She knelt and placed her head on the block.

Maddalena turned and fled toward the Tower entrance, unable to remain near the scene. She flinched when she heard the swordsman's stroke and the gasp of the crowd.

The Maddalena turned her face toward the stone wall and sobbed for the woman she did not like and for Anne's three-year-old daughter Elizabeth playing with her wooden dolls, unaware that she was now motherless and her future very much in question.

Moments later, the Duke of Richmond brushed past her. He looked pale and sickened. Henry would be angry to know that his son showed weakness. She rested her hand on his shoulder. For a brief moment their eyes met, but they said nothing. What was there to say? She handed him her handkerchief, and he dabbed at his face. "The secret is ours to keep," she told him. She knew that he abhorred it as she did, but he was as helpless as she.

Maddalena had come to despise the king who didn't have the stomach to attend the execution but sent this boy instead. Was it to toughen him up? Or maybe it was to throw some of the blame onto his son in the eyes of the spectators. Possibly it was a warning to the duke that no one dare be a threat to the king. Not even his son.

King Henry had locked himself in his chambers. He emerged on the second day to marry Anne's maid of honor, Jane Seymour.

Anne wasn't the only one to die; four nobles climbed the bloody steps after making tortured confessions to dalliances with the queen. Some said they had been forced to lie and sacrifice themselves to justify Anne's death and save England.

No one spoke aloud about it, but something was happening, something that Maddalena noticed. The road that slashed through the town of Windsor bore hordes of horse traffic. Hunting parties, the people said. Knights and manor lords, their banners unfurled on staffs, ambled along toward Warwickshire, where the land was rich with animals and fish. It was also the home of Lady Elizabeth Clinton, revered as the mother of the king's son.

The country teemed with unrest. They apparently didn't give one shilling's worth about the royal bloodbath, but they seethed over Henry's continuing efforts to demolish or tax into nonexistence the abbeys and small churches. They also hated his increased demands on the manor lords. The more money and grain he collected from them, the less they had to share with their farmers.

There was tension in the air, and there was a hint of treason. Were the nobles really hunting? Or were they meeting in secret caucuses, planning a rebellion? The duke was so much more popular than his father. And Lady Clinton was equally popular and powerful. Her young husband was dynamic and ambitious. Did they dare commit treason?

Henry sent the duke back to the St. James Castle to resume his studies. Perhaps he knew of the rumors and wanted him out of sight and out of mind. The thing about power, Maddalena realized, was that once people held it in their hands, they could not let go, even for the greater good. That was true whether it was a king or a father. Maddalena wondered if she would ever see the duke again. She would be sorry if she did not, but she fully intended to leave this barbarous country at her first opportunity.

The summer was as hot as the winter had been cold, and the visitors from Venice and even Turin were sparse. Word had no doubt reached them that the king grew more irrational and unpredictable with each day. It was as if a cloud of doom had descended upon Windsor.

The light drizzle turned to a hard rain, and Maddalena slipped past the horses tied to the posts outside the King's Arms Inn. Soaked through and through, she stepped inside to wait until the rain slowed. The sharp odor of the straw on the floor and the sour smell of boiling cabbage assaulted her nose. A small band of well-dressed nobles, no doubt the owners of the fine horses outside, hovered around the fire, drying off. The youthful bard she had seen at the New Year's festivities strummed on a lyre and sang:

> *Sweet Bess did win the heart of the king.*
> *Into the Court a child she did bring.*
> *The golden-haired lad she did bring,*
> *A lad who would someday be king.*
> *Then came new Queen Anne*
> *With her potions so cruel.*
> *And the golden-haired lad*
> *Will never rule.*
> *The lad will never rule.*
> *The devil may have Anne's body.*
> *The king did have her head.*
> *The king did have her head.*

As he sang the last words, the men broke into laughter. Maddalena covered her ears and fled back to the hovel she shared with Alice. Had the country fallen so out of control that they dared to air such treasonous thoughts aloud? Life, even their own, meant nothing to these people.

She could not disregard the heavy feeling of impending doom that seemed to smother her. Her heart leaped at the sudden pounding on the door. Maddalena opened it with dread to find soldiers.

16

Cabot Falls, Vermont
Present Day

*T*he Halloween-themed bridal luncheon was upon Sofia, and she carried the food, decorations, and cake with the pumpkin-head bride and groom to her SUV.

She followed the directions to the upscale neighborhood, a gated community, and stopped at the entrance to give her name to the guard. The metal gate slid open and Sofia eased the Suburban over the speed bump, praying that it didn't send a pumpkin head rolling off the cake.

She paused in front of the mansion with a cluster of black and orange balloons anchored to the mailbox to double-check the address. The Federal-style brick residence spread across what would have been three lots in Sofia's neighborhood. She smiled ruefully, remembering how she'd quoted the lowest possible price because the girl had sounded so naïve.

She turned into the driveway and parked in front of the three-car garage in the rear. One stall was empty. A white convertible sports car and a Cadillac Escalade occupied the other two spaces. Their combined worth was more than the Parkers owed on their house.

The rear door was flung open, and Gretchen yelled, "Boo!" She was, as Sofia had expected, still a teen. What she hadn't expected was that she'd be dressed as Wonder Woman. "Oh, this is such fun. I'm so excited!" the girl said.

A bewildered-looking woman with butterfly wings strapped onto her back shook hands with Sofia and introduced herself as Sharon Wingate, Gretchen's mother. "I hope you're up for this," she apologized. "I really should have followed up on it, but it's time she took responsibility for her commitments. I still have stale cookies in the pantry from her scouting days."

"Oh, well, you should be proud," Sofia said. "She handled it well." Sofia might have thought Gretchen was a tad immature, but she couldn't help but feel for the teenager who had visibly deflated at her mother's words. And yet, Sofia also felt a renewed appreciation for her own helpful, responsible daughters.

Sofia retrieved the linens from her SUV with Gretchen following like Pat's poodle.

"Angie is going to love this," the girl said. "You are so right-on with this."

Mrs. Wingate turned to her daughter. "Why don't you put the tablecloths on the tables?" When Wonder Woman left, her mother sighed audibly. "I can only pray that Gretchen doesn't marry for a long time. And that she picks a month like August."

"August?" Sofia asked.

"Yes, no holiday themes."

Not long after they had finished setting up, costumed guests started arriving. Soon the house was brimming with Cinderellas, Snow Whites, and pirates, sounding like a gaggle of geese. Sofia sliced the rosa di Parma tenderloins and arranged them on a platter. She tossed the salad and scooped the scapece pumpkin with pasta into a wide-mouth orange bowl next to the basket of soft breadsticks.

Sofia used the cake as the centerpiece and retired to the kitchen as Mrs. Wingate called the giggly guests to fill their plates. The noise level decreased considerably, and Sofia figured that her menu was a hit. The lull gave her a chance to try and puzzle through what she had learned yesterday. Borasino had arrived in Cabot Falls after the first problems began. Even his office confirmed that he had been in Montpelier then. Officer Quimby said that the tread on the rental car did not match the tread he photographed in front of her house.

What did Borasino want? Who was he working for?

She shifted in the kitchen chair, biting her lower lip. She couldn't think of anything in her past that would warrant investigation, so maybe it was something from the present—but what? *The present! Of course!*

Suddenly, Sofia could see in her mind's eye her sweet husband hunkering over the calculator. Every so often, Jim checked out the current mortgage rates and figured out if they'd be better off refinancing at a lower rate or if they should hold. He had checked into it a couple of weeks ago. Borasino was probably investigating them for the mortgage company.

It would be natural for the company to verify that they were qualified for a refinance. That didn't sit well in her thoughts, though. If they were already keeping up with their higher payments, wouldn't that be a sign they were good for a lower payment?

She glanced at her watch. It would be Jim's lunch break. He'd be in the teacher's lounge by now. She dialed his cell phone. When he answered, she said, "Jim, I think I know what that detective is doing snooping around on us. I bet it's for the bank holding our mortgage. They do that for loans and sometimes for life insurance, don't they?"

"Not unless the broker is a mind reader, Sofia. I ran the numbers and figured the difference wasn't enough to even think about refinancing. I didn't call the bank."

The buoyancy Sofia had felt only moments before now deflated like a pierced balloon. Borasino was dogging them for some other reason. And what about the difference in tread marks? That meant that there was more than one dark SUV.

Just how many people were following them?

Windsor, England
Summer 1536

Maddalena stared at the soldier before her. It was as if time and her heart stood still as she waited for him to speak.

"The Venetian ambassador requests that you accompany me to his quarters," he said.

She felt her whole body relax. "He's here? Oh, yes. Yes!" She turned to Alice. "This is it. I am going home, Alice."

The stricken expression on the woman's face shocked Maddalena, and she gave her a quick hug before stepping out and closing the door. She felt light of foot, like skipping. She wanted to hug everyone she saw on the way, but she smiled and greeted them instead.

The secretary ushered her into the ambassador's inner office, and he smiled back at her. "I have been asked to deliver in person this correspondence. I understand that it is very good news for you."

She recognized her father's bold, sprawling handwriting and broke the seal to open the envelope quickly, unfolding the letter within. It was dated a month before.

> *You are a fortunate young woman. Signore Damiano Moretti, a well-established owner of a successful glass manufacturing company and recently widowed after ten years of blissful marriage, has agreed to overlook your history of insolence and make you his bride.*
>
> *He has four children you will be expected to bring up in the way he sees fit, and you will oversee his household*

staff. I will expect you to accompany the ambassador on his return and prepare for the ceremony. By my orders, the ambassador will not allow you to join his caravan if you do not agree to the marriage.

I have enclosed a rendering by a local artist of Signore Moretti so that you may recognize your groom.

Maddalena could feel the rage building in her. Her temples throbbed and her throat tightened. She crumpled the letter angrily and was about to crumple the sketch without looking when something caught her attention. The artist's signature: Allessandro Addonzio. Did her father's cruelty know no limits? Had he commissioned her only true love to sketch some stranger she was to marry? Why would Allessandro agree to do it?

The folds of the garment seemed askew, and the shadows were all wrong. Allessandro was incapable of such shoddy work. It was deliberate. Yes, the darker areas were clearly her initials. She smiled.

The ambassador obviously thought that she was pleased with the offer. "Then you will be ready to travel in two days?"

Maddalena stood. "You can tell my father that when I return to Venice, it will be on my own terms, not his. Good day, Signore Ambassador." She spun on her heel and flung open the door to the waiting area. With barely a glance at the startled secretary, she left the ambassador's quarters and exited the building as quickly as she could. She leaned against the outer wall, sucking in deep breaths. No tears came. There was only determination and resolution. "My own terms," she repeated to herself. "Mine alone."

She hurried to the palace and the sewing room. For now there were clothes for the rapidly growing little Elizabeth. She wanted to make them especially pretty for the little princess, but not royal blue. She could not erase the vision of Anne's last dress from her mind.

Alice looked up as she entered and smiled. "I knew you'd come back."

"For now, Alice." She would bide her time. She knew that Allessandro would wait.

Time seemed to stand still, but at last she received word that the captain of a sailing ship, *Bright Star,* had accepted her as a passenger if she was ready to board in a week's time. At his insistence, she sent her fare by a village boy and agreed to make up the rest by working in the galley and keeping his quarters clean. She decided not to tell Alice or the others until the last moment possible. It would take two days to reach Dover, where the ship was moored. That gave her five days to complete Elizabeth's dress.

Then, two days before her departure, she received a note from Henry Howard, requesting her presence at St. James Castle in London. He asked on behalf of his friend and brother-in-law, Henry Fitzroy, Duke of Richmond.

Maddalena thought it odd that it was not the duke himself who made the request, but she accepted eagerly. She was glad to be able to see her friend before she embarked for Venice.

"A carriage is waiting in the courtyard," the footman told her. "If you will come with me now, please."

It was a shiny black carriage with four matched ebony jennets. Maddalena felt like a princess, stepping up into the cab of black leather. She was aware of her coworkers' faces peering from their window. She leaned out of the cab and waved.

St. James Castle was every bit as impressive as Windsor Castle. She swiveled her head from one side to the other, drinking in the rich sights of luxurious furniture, art, and highly polished silver and gold wherever she looked.

She followed Henry Howard up the stairs to private quarters. The anteroom was as richly furnished as those meant for public view. The mahogany desk was stacked high with books. Next to them was a globe. Maps of the heavens, Europe, and Asia and an intriguing one labeled "New World" adorned the walls.

Wordlessly, Henry Howard opened a heavily carved door. Maddalena walked past him into the bedroom, where an imposing canopied bed dominated the room.

Were it not for the familiar smile, she might not have known the young figure reposing there. "Your Grace?"

"Maddalena. You came. Thank you."

"Oh, Your Grace, you . . ." She couldn't find the words. He was pale and thin, and in the dim light, he looked almost wizened.

"I have not known you to be at a loss for words, Maddalena. I must look worse than I feel." His voice lacked the strong confidence, the cheeriness that was so endearing to her.

"Oh no, Your Grace," she lied. Inside, her heart felt torn apart. "I was just—just surprised to find you taken abed. That's all."

"Stay, Maddalena." He leaned forward, wincing in obvious pain. He rubbed his abdomen.

"Of course," she said. "The day is young."

"I mean live here. See me through this. I trust you. You are a true friend."

Maddalena slumped into the chair by the bed. "Live here? What of your wife, Your Grace?" She was touched that he considered her a friend, as she felt the same of him. Their worlds were so different, yet they did have much in common. It puzzled her that she was preferred over his peers. But she understood. He was trapped with a cold woman who didn't love him and her brother.

"Mary lives in another wing. Everyone seems to have

disappeared except to bring meals. The king's physician comes. But no one comforts me like you, Maddalena, even when you are challenging me. Will you stay?"

She realized there was but one answer to that. He was her friend. God willing, she would see him back to health. She would not be on the *Bright Star* when it sailed. Only her year's wages would make the journey. But she owed him her life. "I will send for my clothes. I will stay in the anteroom so that I might hear if you call out." He need never know what she'd sacrificed.

As the days rolled into a week and then another, Maddalena sat at the duke's bedside, reading to him or telling him of her Venice. "Oh, Your Grace, you would love the *Masques Carnevale*. The streets fill with costumed people. The gondolas are decorated with ribbons and flowers. The bridges are decorated with lights and ribbons. And oh, how we feast! We store up like squirrels for winter, and then we observe Lent until the *Pasqua* feast. Families forget their petty squabbles to unite in the celebration of Easter."

While he slept, she thought of her beloved country as she embroidered olive leaves on a square of pale green silk she had saved.

The duke grew weaker. She brought him soup and tea and cider, but none of it helped. He seemed to shrink with each day passing.

It was the third week when he asked her for pen and paper. With great effort, he sat up and wrote, sealing the envelope with candle wax and pressing into it with the ring he wore. "You are a good friend, Maddalena, rarer than the most precious gems. God bless your kind spirit." He handed her the envelope. It was addressed to Lady Clinton. "You will know when to deliver it, Maddalena."

She could not stop the tears that leaked from her eyes and rolled down her cheeks. "Please, no, Your Grace. Don't talk like that."

He smiled weakly. "Open the drapes, Maddalena, so that I might look upon the sun. Go outside and sit in the garden awhile. It will do you good."

"I can stay with you, Your Grace. Let me help you to the window," she begged. She felt as if her heart were being squeezed. She could barely catch her breath.

"I'm tired, Maddalena. Go now. And thank you."

She sat in the garden. It was the third week in July, and only the hardiest of blooms remained in the heat. The sun was muted by light haze. She watched as a crow pecked at the ground, pausing to cock its head and look at her intently. Crows were harbingers of death according to the old crones who bustled about the palace. They chased them away. Yet when pain became too unbearable, did one welcome the crows? A shiver traveled up her spine despite the heat. It was time to rejoin the duke. Today she would tell him how the sun on the water looked like diamonds and how the lagoon at night brought the stars down so close that you could touch them.

She clutched her cross necklace as she ascended the stairs and whispered a prayer that soon the duke would rally to health.

As she entered his quarters, the king's physician brushed past her, pausing briefly as their eyes met. He said nothing, but she knew. Alarmed, Maddalena rushed into the bedroom. The duke's body lay lifeless beneath a white linen shroud. Her lips numbed and her vision blurred. She reeled dizzily and her legs turned to pudding. Everything went dark as Maddalena crumpled to the floor.

17

Cabot Falls, Vermont
Present Day

$\mathcal{S}$ofia crumpled her latest shopping list and tossed it into the basket, satisfied that it had served its purpose and all items were present and accounted for. She startled as Jim asked, "You okay? Have you found out any more about why that detective is asking about us?"

"I'm hounding poor Ryan Quimby to get the answers. If he doesn't call soon, I'll sic Pat on him." She grinned at the thought. "I'm afraid that we are back to square one about the notes, though. They preceded Borasino's arrival. I hope that it's just some ill-conceived prank."

Luke came in. "What can I eat?"

"There's sliced roast and sandwich fixings in the fridge," Sofia replied. "Have you decided on a costume yet? Time's running out."

"I'm not wearing one. It's for little kids."

Shaking her head in dismay, Sofia said, "Everyone dresses up—kids and adults. Why don't you want to this year?"

"Twelve-year-olds need our dignity, Mom."

Sofia shrugged, although she saw his point. "If you change your mind—"

"I won't." Luke slapped the second piece of bread on top of his sandwich and walked off.

"I can understand," Jim told her. "I'm going as Wyatt Earp, Sofia. No tights for me."

"Men. Read your history, Jim. There was nothing ladylike about those men."

Before Jim could defend his position, the phone rang. It was Officer Quimby. "Mrs. Parker, I've had a talk with Sam Borasino, and he's on the up-and-up."

Sofia balled her fist as she spoke. "There is nothing legitimate about following us or snooping around our neighborhood to ask people about us. Are you sure that he got into town only a few days ago? Maybe he was driving a different vehicle at first. Have you checked registrations at all the places to stay?"

Quimby audibly sighed into the phone. "Mrs. Parker, I assure you that he is on legitimate business."

"If he's legitimate, then he should come to our door and ask questions to our faces instead of skulking around and riling up our neighbors who must think goodness-knows-what about us now."

"He's looking at you and your husband in connection with a man named David Dyer. Sound familiar?"

"No, not at all." She cupped her hand over the speaker and asked, "Jim, do you know a David Dyer?"

Scowl lines creased his forehead and his lips tightened in a thin straight line. He shook his head no.

"Who is this Dyer person?" Sofia asked the officer.

"He's a local felon who was recently released from prison."

Sofia gasped. "If this detective thinks we're involved with a criminal, then he's not a very good detective."

"Yes ma'am. I told him that to all appearances, you folks are good citizens living ordinary lives. But he has to figure this out for himself."

Sofia steadied herself against the counter. "Well, in this

case, appearances are the reality. This felon must be the actual stalker, right?"

"He fell off the grid the minute he stepped outside the prison gates. He has family here, but they haven't seen him."

"Isn't he supposed to report to a parole officer or something?"

"Not in this case. He served his full sentence—no time off for good behavior."

Her heartbeat quickened as the notes flashed into her head: *Danger! You were warned!* "You mean he's dangerous?"

"Oh no, ma'am. The warden says he was a model prisoner. He was denied parole because he refused to cooperate with authorities in their investigation."

"Into what?"

"It was a jewelry heist about ten years ago. The loot was never recovered. But they had his prints and his mug right there on camera. He confessed and waived trial, but he kept quiet about the circumstances."

"Why would Borasino think that *we* know where this guy is?" Sofia said.

"He insisted he had his reasons," Officer Quimby said. "The best I can do is to look out for Dyer. If he shows, I can warn him not to harass you. And I can't interfere with Borasino's investigation unless he does something illegal."

After the call ended, Sofia repeated to Jim what Quimby had said. "I am more angry than afraid, Jim. This Dyer could very well be the real stalker. But why us?"

Later that night, Sofia had finally managed to chase the questions into a corner of her mind and fall into a shallow sleep when she was startled awake by Jim's shout.

He sat bolt upright in bed. "I know who Dyer is, and I know what our connection is to him."

Sofia leaned against the headboard and braced herself.

London, England
Summer 1536

Maddalena fought consciousness until the physician's offensive-smelling salts forced her to accept it. She had to face the fact. The duke, son of King Henry VIII and Elizabeth, Lady Clinton, lay dead at seventeen.

Youthful death was not uncommon in England. Disease and accidents claimed many. But only weeks before, Henry Fitzroy had been a robust and healthy youth. There was no fever, no sweating sickness. In her three weeks at the castle, all the nourishment he consumed should have given him strength. Instead, he had grown weaker each day.

Maddalena stood up and straightened her skirt. She would mourn her friend in time. She would pray for his soul. But for now there was work to be done. *The letter.* "You'll know when it is time to deliver it," he'd told her. Did he know then that he soon would be dead? How does one really know? She remembered that he'd set the letter on the side table.

The door to the bedroom was closed, and she opened it and went in. She kept her eyes down, looking at the Oriental rug on the floor. She could not bear to see the shroud there covering his body.

The letter was not there.

Perhaps Duke Henry Howard had left to give it to Lady Clinton, saving her the pain of performing such a sad errand. She went to the downstairs parlor where the Howards had gathered. "The duke had a letter on the table," she said.

"You are mistaken," the physician said. "There was no letter."

"Begging your pardon, but I am not mistaken. I witnessed him writing it myself. He asked that I deliver it to his mother." She returned his stare. "I intend to deliver it as I promised, or to inform Lady Clinton of its disappearance."

Henry Howard stood. "She is correct, doctor. I . . . I believe it is here at the writing desk." He handed it to Maddalena. "She is at her home in Warwickshire. You had best put it in the hands of her parents, Sir John and Lady Catherine Blount. Let them have the responsibility of getting it to her. And since you are returning to Windsor, you may deliver this message to the king, also." He handed her a second missive.

"The king?" Maddalena asked meekly. She remembered the stories of the Greeks, and the phrase "kill the messenger" came to mind. "Shouldn't one of you as his kin be more appropriate?"

"You are in no position to tell us what is appropriate," Henry Howard said. "Do as we tell you, and wait for a reply. We must know what the king wants us to do with the body."

Maddalena took the two notes and stood at the portico, awaiting the carriage. Not an hour ago he was Duke of Richmond, son of the king, and now he was "the body" to them. His widow, Mary Fitzroy, was absent from the family gathering. Was that because she was closed away, grieving? Or was it because she was as callous about his death as she had been about his days of illness?

Maddalena tried to prepare herself on the ride to Windsor. She felt as if she were in some unreal play, that soon the curtain would fall and she'd be free to go about her life. Windsor came into view. She whispered a silent prayer that she could keep her wits about her.

Someone of such lowly esteem would not be permitted beyond the scribe's desk, for which Maddalena was grateful. She did not want to hand such a note to the king. Apprehensive, she waited as instructed.

From beyond the closed door there was silence at first, and then came a cry so anguished and heart-chilling that she could compare it to no other she'd ever heard. No matter the plotting and planning, no matter the infants bearing the Tudor name that lay entombed, Henry Fitzroy was the king's son, his future beyond his own grave. Silence followed. Nothing but silence. A king must show no weakness, even in the depths of grief.

The door opened, and the scribe, looking pale and pained, sat wordlessly at his desk and wrote a brief note. He sealed it with the Tudor rose stamped into wax and handed it to her, shaking his head slowly.

"I have a note to Lady Clinton from her son," she said. "Will you see that it gets into the hands of her father, Sir John?"

She wanted to rush through the castle to tell her sewing companions, but the carriage was waiting. She was not through with her duties yet. Maddalena dreaded returning to the castle of the Howard family. She felt uneasy with them. Their reaction to the duke's death was disturbing.

Was he not Mary Howard's husband, even if only in name? And Henry Howard had grown up with Henry Fitzroy, playing, studying, and competing. Had he not been still living among them?

Back at St. James Castle, the carriage paused under the portico. Maddalena stood looking out over the grounds for a moment. Gardeners were hunched over, pulling weeds, unaware of the drama within. A lone horse stood saddled at the post. There was no hint that change was in the wind.

She found Henry Howard with his father and handed the note to the elder Howard. He read it and tossed it onto a small round table. Motioning to his son, the elder Howard stalked from the room and out of sight. Maddalena waited, and when no one returned, she read the note:

*King Henry VIII wishes for you to seal the duke's
corpse in a metal coffin and leaves the disposal to you.*

She felt as if the king had driven a knife through her heart.
Was this the wish of the man who had bellowed in such anguish?
Had he gone completely mad? Surely they would understand that
he was in shock.

I must get away from this place. She felt little welcome at the
castle anyway, except to spare them the duke's needs. She dashed
up the stairs and gathered her clothes. As she finished, she heard
a horse whinny. Perhaps the carriage was ready to return her to
Windsor. She looked out the window.

"No!" She beat on the windowpane with her fists. "Stop!" She
pushed, trying to open it, but she could not budge the latch. Two
men dressed in drab peasant clothes unceremoniously dumped
the duke's shrouded body into the bed of a hay wagon and covered
it with straw. There was no sealed metal coffin—no coffin at all.
She dashed down the stairs and out of the castle.

Grabbing the reins of the waiting horse, she mounted and dug
in her heels, urging him forward. The horse broke into a trot and she
struggled to remain upright. The wagon had made some distance,
and she made no effort to catch up. She decided to follow them.
What were they up to? Surely they had summarily disregarded
the Howards' orders. Or had the Howards disregarded the king's?

Maddalena reined in the horse as the wagon turned toward
Thetford Priory and the cemetery that bordered it on one side.
The two men left the wagon and dug a shallow grave outside the
gated wall that surrounded the cemetery. She gasped as they lay
the figure wrapped in white in the grave and shoved dirt over it
until the ground looked flat.

Stunned, she watched as they turned the wagon around and
headed her way. She was tempted to block their path, to turn them

around immediately and demand that they give him a proper burial. Instead, she averted her gaze. She could not bear to look on the faces of these calloused men. They had treated the young duke as if he had died of the plague.

Maddalena felt tears splash onto her cheeks. He was buried in unconsecrated ground with no abbot, no monk, and no priest to pray. There was no mourner at the grave site. Nothing.

She urged the horse forward to the site. Maddalena knelt at the freshly turned earth. She said a prayer. When she had finished, she said, "My sweet, kind prince, I will keep you in my heart always." She removed the cross from around her neck and jammed it into the soft dirt. She covered it, fearing the glint of the sun on it might attract attention.

The church bells were silent. There were no men of the cloth about and no one in the cemetery to see. The road was empty. Maddalena remounted and turned the horse toward St. James Castle. She let the horse plod slowly. Her heart was heavy, but her blood raged through her body. She had to tell them what she witnessed so that they could rectify it.

It was late afternoon. She saw no one in the public areas and she went up the stairs to retrieve her clothes. The cot she had slept on was already removed. The bed linens were gone from the four-poster bed. Henry Howard sat at the desk and looked up as she entered.

"The carriage is waiting to take you back to Windsor. Your service here is over," he said.

"I am ready, but before I go, I must sadly report what I witnessed. The two men of your employ did something so horrible that I can barely make myself describe it."

"Oh?" Howard shoved back his chair and stood to face her. "You saw something?"

She described in detail what she had witnessed, omitting her own actions. Her instincts told her to wait to gauge his reactions.

"I am so sorry to have told you. But I—"

"You saw nothing," he said. "Do you understand? Nothing." His voice seemed low and hollow, as if spoken from the bottom of a well. It was so emphatic, so sinister, that she stepped back in shock.

Maddalena swallowed hard. "Maybe I was not clear, but I did witness this blatant disrespect of the king's wishes for his son. His son! If only you'd heard for yourself his reaction to the news, you would know that this will crush him beyond—"

Henry Howard grabbed her arm so tightly that pain shot into her shoulder. "Listen to me, you silly girl. The king's wish was that we handle the disposal as we saw fit. He wanted no part of the arrangements."

"Let go," Maddalena said. "You're hurting me!"

He let go of her arm, but the marks of his hand remained. "You will forget what you saw. You will not speak of it again. It is none of your business. It is best that no one know of this. It is for the king's protection that we do this. It is for your protection that you forget. Now, the carriage is waiting. Go."

Maddalena stared at Henry Howard in disbelief. Forget? His protection? Her protection? Was that a veiled threat? Dare she do what she knew was right? If she did, might she end up in a shallow unmarked grave too?

18

Cabot Falls, Vermont
Present Day

Sofia flicked on the bedside lamp, bathing the rosy walls in a honey glow. The light reflected off four baby pictures on the opposite wall. "Okay, I'm ready. Hit me with it," she said. After these last few weeks, she doubted anything could shock her anymore. "How do we know a convicted felon, a jewel thief?" The night chill had settled in. Sofia grabbed her robe and wrapped it around her shoulders.

Jim reached for her hand. "I thought the name sounded a little familiar, but I couldn't place it until now. Remember that I reviewed the mortgage a few weeks ago?"

"Yes, but you said we wouldn't gain anything by refinancing. I remember. You also said that you didn't contact the bank."

"No, but I remember the name Dyer from the mortgage papers. The house was constructed in 1950 by Dyer Construction Company," he explained. "Dyer was the original owner and seller."

"Okay, but that was over sixty years ago, before either of us was born. The house went through two owners before we bought it."

Jim got out of bed and paced back and forth as he related his memory. "When we added the four-season room ten years ago, the company was still in business. Still family owned. I knew that I could do the framework and the drywall, but I didn't trust my skills with the electrical work or the leak proofing where the new room attached to the original house. Dyer's company still had the original house plans on file, so I hired them to do what I couldn't."

Sofia cut through the cobwebs of her mind. "What does any of that have to do with what's happening now?"

Jim yawned. "I have no idea. But at least I can sleep now that I know that much." He turned out the bedside lamp and quickly settled into a soft snore.

Sofia tossed her robe onto the rocker, turned off the light, and pulled the covers up to her chin. She tapped Jim on the shoulder. "Roll over."

Jim turned on his side, and his snoring stopped.

"Thanks a lot," she whispered. "Now I've got all those questions swimming around in my head again."

Sofia realized that her opportunity to sleep had passed. Thoughts collided in her brain. Other than this house, what connected them to a jewel thief? What did Borasino know that they didn't? Could Officer Quimby be holding something back? He had said that things were not always how they appeared. Was he referring to Borasino, Dyer, or maybe the stalker?

She slid on her fleece-lined slippers and descended the two flights of stairs to the computer in the basement. She looked up the Dyer Construction Company. The article said that Douglas Dyer, a veteran of World War II, started the company, remaining active until 1985, when his son, Dillon, took over. He must have been with the company when Jim hired them.

David Dyer was probably Dillon Dyer's son—from pillar of society to felon in three generations. If there had been a jewelry robbery, it would have been reported on.

After the family left for school, Sofia returned the borrowed books to the library.

"I haven't absorbed everything I read, but I got a lot of insight into life with Henry," she told Marla. "But I'm here for the turn of the century."

"Anything in particular?" Marla asked. She walked toward the back. Sofia fell into line behind her, keeping pace.

"I'm looking for the news coverage on a jewel theft and especially a thief named David Dyer. I think it was around ten years ago." That year brought back so many memories. Matthew had been born in June, right in the middle of building the room addition.

"Here it is," Marla said. She pointed to the news headline: *Quarter-Million Jewelry Heist Suspect Confesses.* There was a photo labeled David Dyer. He looked a great deal like his grandfather. The article said that Dyer confessed to the robbery but refused to reveal the location of the jewelry. The insurance company issued a statement that they would never give up on recovering stolen items.

She read further that the burglar alarm summoned the police and there had been a chase. They lost him. When they caught up with him several days later, the jewelry was missing, never to be seen again.

London, England
Summer 1536

It was upsetting to Maddalena how kin and lifelong friends could be so callous, although she probably should not have been surprised, given her treatment by her own father. But Henry

Fitzroy was the heir to the throne—the only son of a king, and a good person. Did that mean nothing?

Maddalena hurriedly tied her clothes into the wool cloth and left. She could not wait to leave this horrible place of heartless people. But forget what she saw? Never. She would shout it from the rooftops. She would force the king to listen. She would . . .

Maddalena shrugged helplessly. What could she really do? They were mighty, and she had no status in this world of madness. Who would listen to a penniless seamstress? She was glad that she had remained with the duke, even though it meant she could not leave England.

She climbed into the waiting carriage and settled into the seat. As it bumped along the rutted road, she gazed out the window. Tenant farmers—men, women, and even children—tended the manor's crops. In their drab clothing, they blended into the scene so that they were nearly invisible. It might have been an illusion, but it was also a truth: They were more a part of the land than the lords, although they would reap little benefit from their work.

She was no different. She'd come to England as a privileged girl, daughter of a wealthy merchant, but she'd learned a great deal about survival from life as a peasant, still more privileged than those working the fields. She had lived in the presence of royalty, nobility, and the struggling poor. One thing had remained clear in her mind through it all: Right is right. And today she had seen something so wrong that it rent her heart.

By now the duke's grandparents had been informed of their grandson's death. They would have sent a messenger in his jaunty uniform bearing the Blount crest, racing his way to Warwickshire to tell their daughter that her firstborn was no more, delivering his message by his own hand to her. Maddalena could not imagine the depth of pain she would feel.

The king's anguished wail echoed in her mind. So grieved at the news, his first reaction was to refuse any part of it. However, leaving the arrangements to the Howard family had been a terrible error in judgment.

Windsor came into view. Her instincts had served her fairly well through her English stay. She hoped that they did not fail her now. The carriage stopped in front of the King's Arms Inn, and she thanked the driver before taking her belongings to Alice's dwelling.

Still puzzling over her dilemma, Maddalena hurried up the hill to Windsor Castle. There she rushed down the corridor toward the sewing room, but she stopped short. The painting of the duke as a small child holding a marmoset, his dapper little plumed hat atop his head, was missing from among the portraits of royalty.

For a moment she thought perhaps she was mistaken. It could be farther down the wall. She slowly made her way along the hall. There were blank spots throughout. Missing were the portraits of the duke as he grew and changed.

Maddalena sought out Hans Holbein, the king's portrait painter. "I thought perhaps one painting was removed for cleaning or to be placed in the king's chambers," she told him. "But all of them are missing. What has happened?"

Hans put his finger to his lips. "*Shh.* It is the king's orders. All of the boy's paintings are to be removed and destroyed."

"Destroyed?" Maddalena gasped. "Has he gone completely mad with his grief?"

"Yes, destroyed," Hans said. "He has forbidden anyone to mention his name. He has promised severe punishment." He paused. "Remember the first time we met, Maddalena? I advised you to stay invisible to the nobles and monarchs as much as possible and to always flatter them. It is the only way to remain safe. Feelings change on a mustard seed here. What was required yesterday can get you hanged today."

Maddalena stood there, hands at her sides, numb. She could hear the words, but she could not get them to make any sense. King Henry had demanded every image of his only son destroyed? Could this be the same man she had heard only hours before, so filled with sorrow and hopelessness that he sounded like a wounded animal? Would it not be more normal, more human, to gather to yourself every memento you could in an effort to hold on to a loved one? Yet he would destroy all vestiges of the son to whom he would have given his kingdom?

She acknowledged Hans's words with a nod and left the studio. How could King Henry command all the paintings of Henry Fitzroy be destroyed? How could he forbid his name to be spoken? Images in memory gradually fade. Even now she couldn't get a clear picture in her mind of her own father. Were it not for her sketches, she might forget altogether. *My sketches!* She had so many sketches of the duke. She had to protect them from all eyes.

She stood outside the door to the sewing room, bracing herself for the unexpected. They had always been curious and full of questions. Would they ignore the king's ban, or would they simply ignore her three-week absence?

She walked in. Alice smiled. "The prodigal daughter returns. Here, sit by me, Lily."

Maddalena smiled at her. She realized it was useless to remind the poor woman that she was not her daughter.

Lucy offered an uncharacteristically subdued welcome. The pall had settled in Windsor. Mabel tossed an unfinished bodice to her. "This needs rows of layered lace. Get to work. There's been enough time wasted."

Maddalena opened her mouth to tell Mabel that time was not wasted when it was in the service of someone ill. But everyone was so frightened. She did not know what had happened in her absence. Perhaps they were more afraid now than ever. The king was unpredictable. Hans's words flooded her thoughts: "Stay invisible." Yet circumstances beyond her control had made that impossible.

The women worked in silence. Maddalena tried to concentrate on the bodice for Queen Jane. Had the king already turned his thoughts of a male heir toward her? Could he forget young Fitzroy and turn to the unknown as easily as he changed wives?

Her thoughts were caught in a whirlwind. So much had happened that she had all but forgotten that only a few short weeks ago, her father had wanted her to marry a stranger. She had not been able to destroy the sketch of her suitor, as much as she wanted to. After all, Allessandro had drawn it. Had she only imagined her initials embedded in the sketch? Or did Allessandro deliberately include them as a message to her?

Three weeks ago, she had celebrated that it was his message that he was waiting for her to rejoin him. Now she was not so sure. What if the message was an approval of the marriage to the signore? What was she to do? She had lost her year's wages in the advance pay to the captain of the *Bright Star*. It would take her another year to try again. Even Allessandro's image had grown dimmer in her memory. Had her own image completely faded from his?

Why was it that every time she believed that she had done the right thing, the human thing, she ended up being punished?

"He's dead." Lucy's voice cut through her thoughts, startling her.

"What?"

"Thom. He's dead. They hanged 'im two weeks ago while you were consorting with the duke," Lucy said.

"Oh. I supposed he would be. It was a terrible thing he did, killing Rose like that," Maddalena replied. She had forgotten about Thom in the turmoil that surrounded her. But was he worse than any of the nobles she had just left? "I was not consorting, Lucy. I was caring for the sick."

She looked out the window. The sun was barely visible above the trees that lined the western horizon. She wondered if the messenger had paused on the road, sparing Lady Elizabeth her angst for one more night. If he trudged on and rousted her from sleep, he would introduce her to a sorrow she would carry the rest of her days.

When Mabel excused them for the night, Maddalena walked with Alice through the corridor, which reflected a pale gold from the lighted candles. She felt as empty as the spaces that once had held the duke's portraits. Secreted in the pocket of her skirt were sketches that honored his memory in a small way, simple drawings for which she could be severely punished.

She could not get the duke's death out of her thoughts. The king could make all the edicts he wanted, but he could not control her thoughts any more than she could. Why did a healthy young man who had shown no signs of fever, no signs of the sweating sickness, simply up and die in the heat of July? The balladeer's words returned: *The lad will never rule.*

How had the singer known something no one else had? Was he privy to some book of fate? He had sung of Queen Anne with "her potions so cruel."

Could it be true? Was Anne really a sorceress who could reach out from her grave and kill the young duke?

Maddalena shook off the ridiculous thought. She did not believe in witchcraft. It was merely something peasants created to explain happenstance and evil deeds. Yet the duke had been young and healthy. After he fell ill, it seemed the more nourishment he took, the weaker he became. What could explain something like that? She would have no answers should the duke's mother wish to speak with her about his last days.

That night she lay on her mat, but sleep did not come. It was as if every wicked thing that had ever happened in her life took form and tormented her, robbing her of any hope of sleep.

She had finally slipped into an uneasy slumber when there was a pounding on the door. "Open up in the name of the king!"

Dazed, Maddalena stumbled to the door and opened it. The moonlight revealed two grim-faced soldiers. One of them spoke. "Maddalena Vitari, you are under arrest by order of King Henry VIII for the murder of the Duke of Richmond and Somerset."

Murder? Maddalena felt limp with fear. Would this nightmare ever be over?

19

Cabot Falls, Vermont
Present Day

The Renaissance Festival was over, and Sofia's booth had been a rousing success. The girls were back from the Harvest Ball, and the carved jack-o'-lantern stood guard on the stoop. The pumpkin puree was ready to make the soup for the school's Halloween Carnival tomorrow. Sofia stretched and closed her eyes, enjoying the sensation of a day well spent.

With her little chicks all safely in the nest, Sofia set the security alarm and fell into bed next to her snoring husband. She prayed that the worry gremlins would let her sleep because she needed to feel tip-top for the carnival, the last major event of October. The cold weather guaranteed that her spiced cider and pumpkin soup would be hits. Everything was coming together. If only she would hear that Dyer had been caught, it would be perfect.

Sofia was startled awake around two in the morning when Fergus sounded the alarm with such fury that it set off every dog in the neighborhood.

Jim flipped on his bedside light and said, "Stay here."

Sofia grabbed her robe. "Yeah, right." She jammed her feet into her slippers and followed.

As they tiptoed past the boys' room, Jim grabbed the baseball bat from the converted umbrella stand. Sofia peeked in to see that the boys were still sleeping soundly. *Amazing.* She took the only thing left in the stand—a lacrosse stick—and crept down the stairs with one hand resting on Jim's back.

Frantic, high-pitched barking rose from the basement. They found Fergus leaping toward one of the hopper windows, barking and growling. The fur on his neck and back stood up.

Jim flipped the light switch, flooding the room with bright light. As he did, Fergus raced past them and up the stairs to a front window and raised himself up on the sill, snarling.

Sofia and Jim followed. They saw taillights disappear around the corner. Sofia knelt and hugged Fergus to her. "Good boy, Fergus. Good boy." He wagged his tail furiously and licked Sofia's face until she let him go.

"You are a good boy," she said as she stroked him. "You chased the bad guy away." Fergus leaned in and graciously took his rewards for protecting the family.

Jim squatted next to her and ruffled the dog's fur. "Nice work, Fergus."

Sofia looked up at Jim. "Dyer's getting bolder."

"We don't know that it was the stalker, or that the stalker is Dyer."

"Why didn't the security alarm go off?"

"My guess is that all of the doors and windows are still secure. If they weren't, the alarm would have sounded." Jim stood and helped Sofia to her feet.

"You're right," Sofia said, hugging Jim as he rubbed her back.

"We can look outside when it gets light and call the police if we find anything," Jim said into the top of her head. "For now, let's go back to bed."

Sofia gave the dog a treat while Jim checked the alarm system. Then they headed upstairs.

Back in bed, Sofia tossed and turned and didn't sleep again. *How can Jim fall asleep so easily?*

The next morning, the quilt was the last thing on her mind as

Sofia trudged to the computer. But her email subject list shocked her wide awake: *Maddalena Vitari*. The letter was from a distant relative, Vittore Addonzio. He had seen her appeal on a genealogy website and offered to share the contents of his heirloom collection of Maddalena Vitari's love letters. Sofia immediately responded, asking him to send her the information.

By the time she had prepared and fed the family breakfast and Jim had assured her that the outside revealed no evidence of a prowler, Sofia had received at least a dozen attachments in her email inbox.

Vittore ended his note saying that Maddalena had been a painter, and that she and her husband had owned a portrait studio in Venice. He told her that the letters were discovered when a small structure was demolished in Windsor, England. Would Sofia like to see a few of her paintings that he had inherited? She saved the attachments and immediately responded that she would love to see the paintings.

For the first time in weeks, she shoved the stalker from her thoughts. *So I'm not the only odd child in the family, preferring to paint what I see than to sew it.* She could hardly wait to read the letters and see the paintings. It would have to wait, though, until after the carnival.

The brisk, cold air guaranteed more customers to the Parker booth than the cold-drink stand across the campus. Sofia was grateful for the warmth of the many layers of her Renaissance costume, particularly the headpiece that kept her ears snug.

She enjoyed seeing the kids and their imaginative costumes. It was the last customer that turned her blood cold. Despite the wide brim of a safari hat shadowing his eyes, she recognized the man as Sam Borasino, the investigator.

"Mrs. Parker? We need to talk."

"At least you've finally come out of the shadows," Sofia snapped. "But you should be after Dyer, not us!"

"David Dyer is in Florida with a cousin and has been since he left prison."

Sofia felt as if a shock wave had traveled through her body.

Windsor, England
Summer 1536

Maddalena drew back from the soldiers in anguish. "*Murder*? Are you completely mad? Alice, wake up and help me!"

"You are to come with us," the older soldier said to Maddalena. His face was expressionless as he roughly grabbed her arm and pulled her outside.

Alice stirred, blinking drowsily at the commotion.

"Alice, tell them I couldn't do it. Tell them, Alice!" Maddalena pleaded. She could hear the blood rushing through her ears. Her temples throbbed. "Tell someone where I am, please!"

"Lily is a good girl," Alice said. "Don't worry, Lily. Mabel will know what to do."

The soldiers shoved Maddalena roughly into a cage atop a wagon and pressed the horses forward at a slow, steady pace. The full moon was still high in the sky, painting the scene in shades of gray and charcoal. She reached for the comfort of her cross necklace and remembered that she had left it at the duke's grave. That simple gesture had tethered her to his death.

This is insane, she assured herself. In the light of day, every-thing would be clear. They would realize how ridiculous this was.

Clouds momentarily obliterated the moon, and Maddalena was unsure where she was. She knew only that this exterior of the castle was unfamiliar. One of the soldiers opened the cage and motioned for her to climb out. She realized it would be foolish to even think about struggling. Her only hope was to wait until she could speak with the authorities and make them understand that she would never harm the duke or anyone else.

They led her through a dimly lit room and into a nearly dark corridor. One guard opened a heavy oak door and shoved her through it, slamming it closed behind her. The audible click told her that she was locked in. She stood in the silence, waiting for her eyes to adjust. Moonlight through a slit of a window cut a sharp white gash through the blackness. The room appeared small. There was no mat, no chair, nothing. The stone floor had a thin covering of loose straw. The stench was nearly unbearable. Something stirred in the corner.

Maddalena stiffened. "Hello? Is someone there? Speak up."

"Meg here. Who are you?"

"I am Maddalena."

"A Spaniard, are you?"

"No, I am Venetian," Maddalena said. "I should not be here."

Meg let out a hollow laugh. "None of us should be here. I'm just here for me beauty sleep. Now be quiet so I can be about it."

Sleep was far from Maddalena's mind. She walked toward the voice and sat on the floor with her back against the stone wall. Her cellmate quickly slipped into a soft snore, and she closed her eyes, trying to sort through what little she knew and understood.

The soldiers said that the duke was murdered. *How do they know?* There had been no time examine his body. The king's own physician had tended to him every day. She flashed on the chilling way he'd looked at her as they passed in the doorway. Did he know even then? She had been with the duke nearly every moment from the time she arrived at St. James Castle. How could it have happened right before her eyes and she not know it?

What transpired in those last few moments when she was in the garden? If it was murder, then understanding why could reveal the true murderer and free her. But who would want to harm such a gentle, kind boy as Henry Fitzroy? He had been friendly, happy, and fair. In their long chats, he'd told her that even as a young child, he tried to be especially good and study hard to spare his whipping boy any pain. Disobedience and laziness ordinarily meant the rod for some poor peasant boy since no one dared lay hands on the king's son. It seemed so barbaric, punishing an innocent for someone else's crime. But was that not what they were trying to do to her? The duke had been kind to her. He had even saved her life.

Fatigue set in as the adrenalin subsided, and Maddalena fell into an uneasy sleep haunted by nightmares. She ran down corridors, shaking each door she came to, looking for a way out, but she could find none. "Papa! Allessandro!"

"Wake up." Meg shook Maddalena's shoulders. "You were yelling. You are interrupting me beauty sleep, Venetian." She huffed and settled back on the floor.

Maddalena stood and stretched. Her legs were stiff, and the muscles felt tight and cramped. She paced the small room, afraid to go back to sleep. The only person in England who seemed to care about her safety was dead. Alice was slipping deeper into her own fantasy world each day. Would she even tell Mabel what had happened?

Clearly, it was up to her to save herself. The only way to do that was to discover who had killed the young man, or to prove that he had died of some unknown natural cause.

She had to think. Less than two months before, the king had accused his queen of trying to poison the duke and his half-sister Mary. *Poison—that had to be it.* It was silent, and if given in small doses, it might have made him appear ill. If each dose remained in his body until it was a large enough quantity, it could be deadly.

She recalled that Lucy had said arsenic was easily obtained. She had called it "the poor man's divorce." There were other poisons, perhaps not so easily administered, like copper, venom of toads, aconite, cyanide, strychnine, and hemlock. Maddalena had learned many things listening to Lucy chatter on about the seedier things in life. As difficult to accept as it was, she had to assume that one of these had killed the duke. He had been sick for only three weeks, even before she arrived.

"Stop pacing," Meg said. "I was here first. You need to show some respect."

"Sorry," Maddalena said. "I think clearer when I can write things down and look at them on paper." She had fallen asleep with her sketchbook in her pocket. "Since I can't see in here, I need to sort things through the best I can."

Meg pushed to a sitting position. "At least think out loud. If I must be awake, let me hear what you are thinking. I guess you are going to say that you didn't do whatever they say you did. It doesn't matter. Someone has to pay for sins against the crown. You are as good as any. At least I stole the potatoes. My only regret is that they were not very tasty."

"I didn't steal potatoes. I am accused of murdering the king's son."

"By my father's beard, I never met a murderer before."

"You still haven't!" Maddalena shouted.

"You'll hang for sure."

"I did not do it. Now hush, and let me think this through." She resumed pacing. "Queen Anne was beheaded seven weeks ago. The duke became ill three weeks ago, a month after his stepmother's death."

"She was a witch, they say. A grave can't stop a witch," Meg said. "Everyone knows that."

Maddalena kicked at the straw in frustration. "I don't believe that nonsense. Someone very much alive did this." Queen Catherine had resented Henry's preference for young Fitzroy over her daughter, Mary. *But she died six months ago.* Had someone loyal to her done it so that Mary could inherit the crown? What about Mary Tudor herself?

Any one of the nobles at St. James, the castle of horrors, was capable. There was Mary Howard, humorless and stoic. She had not visited her husband during his illness, but she might have servants loyal to her or to the money she could offer.

"George Boleyn!" Maddalena exclaimed. "He was Queen Anne's brother. With her death, he lost his chance to be part of the inner circle of the throne. He might have done it for revenge, or so his niece Elizabeth would inherit the throne."

"Didn't you know he's dead as well? He lost his head two days before the witch." Meg yawned. "You tell a very boring bedtime story. No dragons or ogres, even."

Maddalena paused at the revelation, but then continued thinking aloud. "Henry Howard had opportunity and motive too. What about his blood loyalty? Would he poison a lifelong friend because of his sister? He was angry with me when I threatened to tell how he went against the king's instructions. He would probably think little of accusing me of murder, perhaps a murder he committed."

Maddalena gasped as she had a new thought. "The king! His motive was stronger than anyone else's. He must be aware of the unrest among his subjects everywhere. His oppression of the Church, his erratic decisions to remove lords from their manors and award the land to someone else—he is not so insulated that he doesn't know how unpopular he is. Everyone has heard rumors of an insurrection. What if his thirst for power was stronger than his love for his son? The duke was still very popular among the people. He could not openly execute his son as he did his queen and many nobles."

"You best keep your thoughts to yourself, Venetian," Meg said. "The sun must be up by now, even if we can't see it. You talked the night away. And you're no closer to an answer than when you first arrived."

Sighing, Maddalena sat down beside her. Meg was right. The young duke by his very birth had enemies, any one of whom had the influence to get away with it. And anyone who would murder him so callously would think nothing of letting someone else pay for it.

"Oh, Meg, all those soups and comforting drinks that I carried from the kitchen to the duke—I could have carried death to him. But I swear I did not know. I loved him like a brother." Her shoulders shook as she sobbed uncontrollably.

It would take weeks for word to reach her father or Allessandro. By that time, it would be too late. How many letters had she sent without response? She could not count on either of them. She had no one to speak on her behalf.

The thought that even unknowingly she might have contributed to her friend's death was something she could not bear to think about.

20

*M*addalena sat on the floor of the stone cell, sketching the dozing Meg in the dim light. She and her cellmate had run out of conversation the first day. The poor girl had little knowledge and even less curiosity.

Maddalena realized that if she didn't keep herself occupied, she would only go over the speculation about the murder of the duke, the numerous people who might have done it, and why anyone would accuse her of such a heinous deed. She could not murder her friend! She'd rather die herself. She heaved a weary sigh. She very well might.

For three days she had endured the stench, the discomfort, and the humiliation of the jailer's taunts and threats. "A pretty little lass dangling at the end of a rope will draw the biggest crowd of the year," he said. "The pretty ones always do." And then he'd made a gurgling sound and laughed heartily.

For three days she had eaten nothing but bread soaked in water. And for three days she had seen no one from her life outside these walls. Forsaken by the only people she called friends, she wondered if they were too frightened to be associated with her, or if Alice had even grasped reality enough to tell them what had happened.

Abandoned by her father and apparently even by Allessandro, she mattered to no one. Her father, she understood. He was ambitious and cruel. He had begun as a young man yearning to possess wealth. Instead, it possessed him. He lost sight of all else. But what about Allessandro? Perhaps not every message had reached him, but surely some of them did. Why had he ignored her pleas? Had he forgotten her? Had he found another?

Maddalena closed her sketchbook. She felt a heavy veil of despair engulf her. How long did she have? How long before she'd be dragged in chains before the council and told of the false accusations? Would anyone speak on her behalf?

She startled as the door to the cell banged open. She could feel her heart pounding in her chest. *Already?* Meg roused from her sleep and stared blearily.

"On your feet. You're coming with me," the guard said.

Hesitantly, Maddalena rose to her feet. She adjusted her cap and straightened her shoulders. If this was it, she would show them no fear, she promised herself.

The sunlight streaming into the outer room was so bright after the dim cell that she blinked many times, trying to adjust to it. As she did, she saw the silhouette of a woman. *Alice?* Maddalena gasped. The woman wore the dark, unadorned clothes of mourning. She recognized her immediately.

"Lady Clinton!" Maddalena broke from the guard and rushed toward her. She stopped short of embracing her. Instead she knelt in front of her, sobbing, "Oh, Lady Clinton, I weep for your loss. It is mine too."

Elizabeth Clinton took her hand. "Sit. Talk to me." She took a chair and waved the guard away.

Maddalena sat opposite her. It was the first time she had met the woman the nobles called Bessie. She had seen her in the painting the duke had in his chambers, but in person she was shorter than Maddalena had imagined. She had pale skin and blond hair reminiscent of her Viking ancestors. The blue eyes that now looked so intently upon her were much like the duke's.

"Your Grace, I loved your son as a brother. I would never harm him. If anything, I owed him my life. I swear by all that is holy that I did not murder him." Maddalena related her own theories about the death, describing the final hours. The pain she witnessed in Lady Clinton's eyes increased the heavy ache she felt.

She ended regretfully by telling her about the disposal of his body. "I offered a prayer of redemption and put my cross with him," she said. "I would never harm him, Lady Clinton, not knowingly."

Lady Clinton had listened intently without interrupting her. Now she sat in silence, and it seemed a lifetime before she spoke. "Read this."

Maddalena recognized the paper. It was the note the duke wrote to his mother. She opened it and read:

Dearest Mother:

I cannot alter the fate that awaits me. I ask only that you remember me kindly as your loving and obedient son. I further request that you see that my friend, Maddalena Vitari, is given passage on the earliest available ship bound for her home in Venice. I wish for her Godspeed and happiness all her days.

Your Son, Henry Fitzroy,
Duke of Richmond and Somerset

She reread the words: *earliest available ship . . . Venice.* "I don't know what to say." The words were unfortunately moot. She was to stand trial and probably hang for the duke's death.

Lady Clinton patted her hand. "I have spoken with the king's coroner. He has rethought his findings. My son died of a lingering natural illness. It is for the common good of England and the crown."

"But—" Maddalena stopped short. "The common good," she said, understanding that Lady Clinton no longer had the crown's protection as mother of the king's son. With the popular young Henry dead, there would be no rebellion on his behalf. The king was left to pursue a legitimate male heir. Lady Clinton could live out her days in solitude with her remaining children.

"If there was no murder, then . . ."

"You are free," Lady Clinton finished her thought. "My son believed in you. I will hold you in my heart always for your friendship with him." She placed a small drawstring velvet purse on the table between them. "Your passage," she said. "The ship *Sunrise* will leave Dover Harbor in three days. I will remain in London until my son is properly entombed at St. Michael's Church in Framlingham by order of the king. My carriage will take you to Dover, but you must hurry. Godspeed, Maddalena Vitari." She turned to leave.

Maddalena suddenly remembered the king's edict to destroy all images of the young Henry. "One moment, Lady Clinton. I have something for you." She tore several of the sketches of the duke from her book and handed them to Lady Clinton. "It will be our secret."

Maddalena stepped out into the sunlight. She turned her face toward the sun, feeling its warmth against her cheeks. She was free, and in three days, she'd set sail for home. There she could face whatever she found. She hurried around the outer walls and through the gate, letting her momentum propel her down the steep hill toward the row of inns and Alice's dwelling.

There was no time to tell Mabel in person or to say goodbye to the others. She would write notes. She had only a few possessions to pack.

Maddalena was taken aback to find Alice at her dwelling. The woman's face looked wild, like that of a cornered animal.

"Alice, I must hurry. I cannot properly thank you for letting me live with you, but I will, I promise. I'll send you a beautiful carnival mask too. How would that be?" She scooped up her hairbrush and the shawl she had made herself from scraps of green brocade. "Or a Venetian bowl. Would you like that? A carriage is waiting for me." She turned around and sucked in her breath.

Alice stood between her and the door, and she was holding a dagger. "I can't let you leave, Lily. I have to take care of you."

"Alice, I am not Lily. Put that down, and step out of the way," Maddalena said quietly.

"I'd rather see you dead than run off with John, Lily."

"Who's John?" Had Alice killed Lily? Or had the girl run away? "I am not Lily, Alice. Talk to *me*. It's me, Maddalena . . . uh, Margaret."

Alice blinked at her, smiling with brief recognition before her eyes lost focus again. "Lily, my sweet daughter, you cannot leave me alone to die. Why do you think I hid all your letters? All of *his* letters?"

"You never posted my letters? But you promised." Maddalena eased herself toward the woman. Her heart was racing.

"I had to. And I had to take his letters to you. I couldn't let him take you, Lily."

"Where are the letters?"

"I hid them."

Maddalena's thoughts reeled. All her letters? Allessandro's letters to her? He had not forgotten her! She edged toward the door. "Look closely at me, Alice. I am not Lily. I am Maddalena."

"Forgive me, Lily. I can't let you go." Alice lunged for her.

Maddalena dropped her bundle and wrestled with the woman, knocking the weapon from her hand. She pinned Alice to the wall, holding her wrists firmly. "Alice, you are in there somewhere, I know. I am not Lily. I am not your daughter. I'm sorry, Alice. I owe you so much. But I don't owe you my life."

She let go of Alice and grabbed her sketchbook. Closing the door behind her, she crossed the alley to the inn. Hastily she wrote a note: *Take care of Alice. She needs you more than ever.* She wrapped the note around several gold coins and left it for the owner to find.

A man stood next to the waiting carriage. He smiled and waved as she approached.

Maddalena blinked. The sun was playing tricks on her. She shaded her eyes, studying the fine figure, tall and erect, dressed in the finest brocades. He wore a beard similar to the style King Henry wore. But the eyes—those beautiful eyes could not be hidden. She burst into a full run, shouting, "Allessandro! Is it truly you?"

Allessandro opened his arms and engulfed her in an embrace.

"Oh, Allessandro, you did come for me! But how? My letters—"

"Letters? I got only one. The ambassador's secretary delivered it to me. Let's go home—together," he said.

"Home," she echoed. It had been so long since she'd dared dream of Venice and of the lagoon that held the images of stars like floating diamonds.

Their lips touched, and in that instant, the years apart vanished like mist on a warm morning.

Cabot Falls, Vermont
Present Day

Sofia motioned for Jim to join her at her Renaissance booth, where she was prepared to question the private investigator. "Mr.

Borasino, I can hardly wait to hear why you think that our family has anything to do with a felon. We're parents. I'm a caterer, and Jim's a teacher."

"Respectable jobs have nothing to do with guilt or innocence, Mrs. Parker." Borasino explained that he had been hired by the company that had insured the stolen jewelry. "I had to be sure that you didn't know the suspect."

"You keep saying 'the suspect.' If it isn't Dyer, then who is it?"

Sofia's cell phone rang. The caller ID said Pat Cooper. "Get home ASAP. The cops are here. There was a B and E. I heard glass breaking and your alarm blaring. Fergus got loose through the broken window. He's okay."

"We've got to go, Jim!" Sofia lifted the cumbersome skirt and ran toward the Suburban, keeping pace with Jim. Borasino was close behind.

The neighborhood was bright as day, with floodlights trained on their home and the surrounding woods. Flashing red lights atop the patrol cars reflected off the pristine white clapboard.

Blue uniforms were everywhere. Fergus broke away from an officer and leaped into Sofia's arms, nearly knocking her to the ground. He licked her face. "How did he get out?" she asked the officer.

"A shattered window at the back. The vandal did some damage. Tore part of the wall down."

"He was looking for something." It was Borasino. He offered his credentials to the officer.

Pat Cooper patted Sofia on the shoulder. "It's going to be all right. The perp is going up the river." She cocked her head toward a patrol car where a bespectacled man with receding hair sat. He looked nothing like the photo of Dyer.

Sofia felt dazed. "What was he looking for?" Suddenly, her head cleared. "The kids! They have no idea why we're gone!" She left Jim at the scene and Fergus with Pat and drove back to the school, wondering how she could prepare the kids to come home to this.

Parking, she imagined the abandoned booth. In her haste, she had let the school down. What she found stopped her in her tracks. Luke and the girls were serving cider and soup. She had forgotten how responsible they were.

She told them what she knew as they loaded the slow cookers into the Suburban. "We can pick up the rest after church tomorrow. Right now, we all need to be home."

At home, Jim had shut the door between the kitchen and the vandalized four-season room. He, Officer Quimby, and Sam Borasino, coffee in hand, sat chatting like old friends. Jim smiled up at her. "It's going to be okay, cara mia."

The children rushed off to comfort Fergus. "Who was that guy?" Sofia wanted to know.

"The jewelry store owner," Borasino answered. "He hired Dyer to fake a burglary so he could have the insurance settlement and keep the jewelry. Dyer realized he was set up. He wouldn't tell Monroe, the jeweler, where he hid the stuff."

Quimby cut in. "We believe Dyer wanted to wait awhile to get it back. But Monroe is close to bankruptcy. He needed money. He threatened Dyer's family if he didn't tell him."

"And he threatened us too," Sofia said. "Oh, that weasel!"

"Yeah, he was hoping to scare you into leaving so he could hunt in your house without interruption."

"Here? You mean that we've had jewels in that wall all along?" Sofia asked.

"Nope," Borasino said. "The police caught him ripping the wall apart. It wasn't there."

Jim said, "When Dyer Construction was finishing our job, they were also building the house one lot away."

Officer Quimby laughed. "Another house. Of course. He got the wrong address."

"Won't your neighbors be surprised when I tell them they're in for a bit of insurance reward?" Borasino said.

"And we're left with unwanted ventilation. Deduction's more than the cost of repair," Jim said. "I'll get on it first thing tomorrow."

"Let me help," Borasino said. "It's the least I can do."

The next morning while the two men worked, Sofia opened an email from Vittore Addonzio. It showed a painting he had inherited from their mutual ancestors, the Venetian painters. It was of a hunting party, and the image was so sharp that she could see brushstrokes and a golden crown barely visible against the central figure's ginger hair. Their pale green clothes were painted in such detail that the leaf embroidery was easily visible. A young maiden with dark hair and olive complexion stood off to one side. Maddalena had painted herself into the scene. In the lower right corner was the signature: M.V. Addonzio, 1537.

Maddalena had served an English king, but she had found her way back home.

Learn more about Annie's fiction books at

AnniesFiction.com

- Access your e-books
- Discover exciting new series
- Read sample chapters
- Watch video book trailers
- Share your feedback

We've designed the Annie's Fiction website especially for you!

Plus, manage your account online!

- Check your account status
- Make payments online
- Update your address

Visit us at AnniesFiction.com